THE FAMOUS FIVE AND THE STRANGE LEGACY

THE FAMOUS FIVE are Julian, Dick, George (Georgina by rights), Anne and Timmy the dog.

When the Five befriend a stranger on a train, they're intrigued by the story of his search for his inheritance which is concealed somewhere in a house in Kirrin. Helping him find the treasure proves to be easy, but keeping it out of the clutches of his greedy cousin involves the Five in an exciting and dangerous adventure.

Cover illustration by Doug Post

Also available in Knight Books:

The Famous Five and the Strange Legacy

A new adventure of the
characters created by
Enid Blyton, told by Claude
Voilier, translated by
Anthea Bell

Illustrated by Bob Harvey

KNIGHT BOOKS
Hodder and Stoughton

Copyright © Librairie Hachette 1978

First published in France as *Du Neuf pour Les Cinq*

English language translation copyright © Hodder & Stoughton Ltd., 1984
Illustrations copyright © Hodder & Stoughton Ltd., 1984

First published in Great Britain by Knight Books 1984
Fifth impression 1989

British Library C.I.P.

Voilier, Claude
  The Famous Five and the strange legacy.
  I. Title   II. Du neuf pour les Cinq.
  English
  843′.914[J]   PZ7

  ISBN 0-340-35337-6

Printed and bound in Great Britain for Hodder and Stoughton Paperbacks, a division of Hodder and Stoughton Ltd., Mill Road, Dunton Green, Sevenoaks, Kent TN13 2YA (Editorial Office: 47 Bedford Square, London WC1B 3DP) by Richard Clay Ltd., Bungay, Suffolk.

CONTENTS

Chapter One

A VISITOR FROM CANADA

'I think I can hear an engine whistling!' announced Dick. 'Yes – here comes our train!'

Georgina Kirrin, who was always known as George, and her cousins Julian, Dick and Anne, were standing on the platform at Newton Woodville station. Newton Woodville was a little town about fifty kilometres from Kirrin, where George lived by the sea with her mother and father. Her cousins usually came to spend their holidays with Aunt Fanny and Uncle Quentin too. Just now, they were all waiting for the train to take them back to Kirrin.

All four of them – or all Five, as they were if you counted George's dog Timmy – had been to Newton Woodville for the day. A boy called John, who was at school with Julian and Dick, was celebrating his thirteenth birthday. It was quite a long way to go for a birthday party, but John was a special friend of Julian's, and the children had all had a lovely time. The party itself was a great success. There had been a grand spread for tea, with sausage rolls and ice-cream and a birthday cake made to look like a football pitch, and afterwards the guests put on an improvised entertainment. One boy stole the show with his clever conjuring tricks, and there were two girls who sang very nice songs.

The four cousins from Kirrin did some good turns too. Julian was an expert juggler, and Anne surprised everyone by playing a tune on the mouth organ. She must have been practising in secret! Then George and Dick put on a fine performance of rope-throwing with a lasso. Lassoing was the two cousins' latest craze, and they had been training in the garden of Kirrin Cottage and out on the beach.

The train came into the station and drew up beside the platform. The Five got into the nearest carriage, and George hurried down the corridor, looking into all the compartments.

'Here – let's sit in this one!' she called out to her cousins. 'It's nearly empty!'

In fact, there was only one other person in the compartment, a young man of about eighteen or nineteen sitting in a corner reading a magazine.

'I say, I hope you don't mind our dog?' Julian asked politely. He always had very good manners.

The young man smiled. He had a frank, open face, thick fair hair and beautiful white teeth. But although he was smiling there was a thoughtful and rather sad look in his eyes.

'No, I don't mind at all,' he told Julian. 'I'm very fond of dogs. What a fine animal!'

That was going rather far, because dear old Timmy was really a bit of a mongrel, but George was pleased to hear him praised. Timmy himself seemed to know that their fellow-traveller liked him. He went over to him, and the young man patted his head.

'There's a good dog!' he said.

Then he went back to his magazine. The four cousins settled down in the compartment and started chattering away. George and Dick were still full of their success with the lasso, and they couldn't stop talking about it.

'Didn't Bernard look funny when he started running round the garden, daring you to catch him?'

'You bet he did! He was really staggered when the lasso *did* fall round him – he *literally* staggered, too, but of course he was on soft grass, so he didn't have far to fall. You were jolly good too, George, making your rope whistle through the air and coil in special shapes. None of the others had ever seen anything like that except in films!'

'I'd been mugging it all up in my book called *How to Use a Lasso!*'

'And we'd done a lot of training, of course.'

Anne smiled at her brother and her cousin. 'You'll be real lasso champions!' she said.

'You haven't seen anything yet!' Dick told his little sister. 'We'll be tremendous experts by the end of the holidays – just you wait!'

'And the cowboys will be coming from the Wild West to take lessons from you,' Julian teased them. He was rather amused to hear the two of them boasting so proudly!

George blushed a little, but she said, 'Well, maybe we aren't *really* such experts yet, but practice makes perfect. And throwing the lasso is such an exciting sport!'

Of course, the young man sitting in the corner couldn't help overhearing what the cousins were saying. There was a slight smile on his lips. Timmy, who obviously liked him a lot, went and put his head on the young man's knees, looking up at him and asking to be patted. The young man rubbed between the dog's ears with the palm of his hand.

'Come here, Timmy!' George called her dog. 'You mustn't bother people! I'm awfully sorry, sir.'

The stranger smiled more widely. 'You needn't call me "sir" – it's not so long since I was a boy like you! And the dog doesn't bother me a bit. As I told you, I'm fond of dogs, and this one seems to know it.'

It was George's turn to smile. She *did* look like a boy, with her short, curly dark hair, and the jeans and jersey she always wore! This was by no means the first time someone hadn't realised that she was actually a little girl.

'My dog's name is Timothy,' she said. 'Tim or Timmy to his friends. I'm George Kirrin, and these are my cousins Julian, Dick and Anne.'

'I'm very pleased to meet you,' said their new friend.

'And I'm not really a boy, though I often wish I was!' George finished. 'My real name's Georgina, but I'd rather you called me George.'

'George is certainly a better name for an expert lasso-thrower,' agreed the young man. 'It's a sport more for boys than girls. Well, now let *me* introduce myself – my name's Peter Darcy.'

'Darcy?' George repeated. 'Somehow that name sounds familiar.'

'I believe it's a local surname in these parts,' their new friend told her. 'There have been Darcys living in a little place called Kirrin, not far from here, for hundreds of years. But my grandfather was the last of the family in England. His name was Edmund Darcy – he died quite recently, and I've come over because he left me his big house in Kirrin. It's called Fairfields.'

'Oh, good!' cried Dick. 'Then we'll be neighbours!'

'George's mother and father live in Kirrin, you see,' Julian explained. 'And the three of us are spending our holidays there too.'

They had noticed already that the young man spoke with an accent that sounded a little bit like an American one, although it wasn't quite the same. Anne ventured to ask, 'Where do you come from, then?'

'I'm from Canada,' the young man told them. 'I've been living in Toronto – but I won't bother you with my life story! It's not a particularly happy one.'

'Oh, but I love stories! Even sad ones,' George exclaimed. 'Do go on!'

'George, you mustn't be rude,' Julian told his cousin.

'She's not being rude at all,' Peter Darcy assured him. 'As a matter of fact, I don't mind talking about Grandfather, if you really want to hear!'

'Yes, please!' said Dick.

Peter Darcy got up to close the door into the corridor. It looked as if he wanted to make quite sure he was alone with his new friends. Then he sat down again and began to tell them his story. They sensed that he was feeling rather lonely, and was glad to talk to someone.

'You see, my father was English, but my mother was Canadian,' he began. 'I was born in Toronto, and that's where I've always lived, though I did come over to England once or twice as a boy, to spend my vacation at Kirrin with my grandfather. Then my parents were killed in a car crash a year ago. Dear old Grandfather came over from England specially for the funeral – he knew it would be a comfort to me to have him there. He wanted me to come straight back to England with him, but I still had one year of school to finish, so I

thought it would be better to stay in Canada for the time being. I didn't want to change schools, and I had some cousins on my mother's side in Toronto who said I could go and live with them. So we agreed that in a year's time I'd come over to my grandfather in England.'

'And were you going to live in Kirrin with him?' asked Anne.

'Yes, in a way, but only in the holidays. I'm going to be a doctor, you see, so I planned to study medicine in London.'

'But things didn't work out as you'd expected?' said Julian, sympathetically. 'Didn't you say your grandfather died recently?'

'Yes, I'm afraid so. Only two months ago,' said Peter sadly. 'He died just as I was getting ready to come over to England and see him again.'

The young Canadian fell silent for a while. The children waited – they had an idea that the most interesting part of his story was still to come. Sure enough, after a few moments Peter Darcy went on again.

'Before Grandfather fell ill, he'd made a will leaving everything he had to me. The last letter I had from him was written in rather shaky hand-writing, and it said, "My boy, I am a rich man . . . richer than your parents ever suspected. And since you wish to be a doctor, my fortune will come in very useful to you. If you can pursue a medical career in the best possible conditions, I am sure you will do a great deal of good in the world. My legacy will help you.'' And to start with, said my grandfather, he was leaving me his house, Fairfields.'

'We know Fairfields quite well,' George interrupted. 'It's not far from Kirrin Cottage, where my mother and father live. We sometimes pass the house when we're out for a bicycle ride.'

'I'm planning to spend the summer there. That will give me time to get acquainted with the countryside around Kirrin again. It's so long since I've been there that I've forgotten a great deal.' Peter smiled at his new friends. 'I'll have to rediscover Kirrin! Perhaps you'll help me – show me round the village, and so on?'

'Yes, of course we will,' George told him. 'We'd be delighted to!'

The four cousins could tell that the young Canadian was feeling rather lonely – he had lost his parents and his grandfather within quite a short time of each other, and now here he was alone in a country he hardly knew. He needed friends, and the children had liked him as soon as they met him. And dear old Timmy had taken to him at once, too – that was always a good sign!

They all began talking, and soon the cousins and Peter Darcy were on the best of terms, and making plans for all the things they could do together in the holidays. George, Julian, Dick and Anne were determined to make their Canadian friend feel at home in Kirrin. They were chattering away excitedly when they were suddenly interrupted.

The train jolted, shook, and came to a halt with a violent shock. There was a tremendous and frightening noise at the same time.

They guessed at once what had happened. Their train had been derailed!

Chapter Two

AFTER THE ACCIDENT

Poor little Anne was thrown to the floor of the compartment. Julian and Peter Darcy picked her up at once. George and Dick were clinging to the door of the carriage. Outside the window, the landscape seemed to be swaying to and fro. Cries of alarm came from the other compartments in their carriage, and the engine was letting out loud, piercing whistles.

Poor old Timmy was terrified, and was barking at the top of his voice.

'Careful!' called Peter Darcy. 'Hold tight, everyone!'

It was as if he had guessed what was going to happen next. Their carriage gave a jerk and then heeled slowly over on its side, like something in a slow-motion film. Probably the carriages in front of it and behind it were breaking its fall.

'Oooooh!' breathed the children, all together.

'Hold tight!' Peter told them again.

'Woof!' said Timmy.

And the carriage landed right on its side, with a tremendous crash of broken glass from the windows.

The travellers had instinctively grabbed at the luggage-racks and the frame of the door into the corridor – anything that would give them something firm to clutch.

Very luckily there wasn't anything heavy in the luggage-rack except for Peter's two suitcases. The suitcases did fall out, but they didn't hurt anyone.

The train had come to a complete standstill. A thick cloud of dust rose from the ground. It got into the overturned carriages, making people cough. The shouting was louder than ever. The Five felt as if they were in the middle of a nightmare.

Julian couldn't see anything for the dust, but he was a very brave boy, and he was the first to move again after the accident. He found that he could stand upright, but his feet weren't resting on the floor of the compartment, because the floor had turned into a wall! He was standing on a grassy slope outside the window – the pane of glass in it had shattered. What a good thing Julian was wearing jeans which had kept his legs from being cut!

The others, who had been sitting or lying among bits of splintered wood and broken glass, managed to get up too.

'Anne, are you all right?' Julian asked his little

sister anxiously. 'And what about you, George and Dick? And you too, Peter?'

They all felt themselves a bit gingerly, quite surprised to find there was nothing much wrong with them.

'I'm all right,' Anne said at last. 'No, honestly, Julian, I'm not hurt, just a bit bruised, I think!' Though she seemed so timid, Anne could really be a very brave little girl.

'I'm all right too,' said George. 'I just got a few bumps – I expect we'll all be black and blue tomorrow!'

Dick had a slight cut on his forehead, Peter's hand was scratched, and one of Julian's wrists seemed to be sprained, but not too badly. Altogether, they thought they had got off lightly.

Dick rubbed his eyes. They hurt with all the dust that had got into them. 'I'm afraid not all the passengers in this train may have been so lucky,' he said. 'There's an awful lot of screaming going on – perhaps some people are really hurt.'

'Then we must see what we can do to help them,' George decided. 'To start with, let's get out of here!'

'I wonder what it was that derailed the train?' said Dick.

'Maybe the points were set wrong,' suggested Peter. 'If we'd collided with anything, the shock would have been much more violent.'

'We were jolly lucky the train was going fairly slowly,' said Julian.

George, who had a practical nature, was already looking for a way to get out of the overturned carriage. That wasn't as easy as you might have expected, because the carriage was lying on its side, so no one could use the door leading directly out of the compartment – and it was difficult to get at the other door leading into the corridor at all! All the glass in the windows on the corridor side had been broken, so getting out of them would be easy enough – but just at the moment they were up above the passengers where the ceiling ought to be, so the real problem was reaching them.

Luckily the four children and their new friend Peter were all quite nimble and athletic. Giving each other a leg up, and using all the hand-holds they could reach, they managed to get out of the carriage and up on its side, which was now its roof! Poor old Timmy was a bit of a problem, and they had to haul him up on the end of George's lasso.

Sitting on the side (or roof) of the carriage, they could see that some of the other carriages of the train had been derailed in the same way too.

'We'd better get down from here as fast as we can,' said Dick.

The lassoes came in useful again. Dick tied his firmly to a window-frame, between two broken panes of glass, and he, Julian, George, Anne and Timmy were soon safely on the ground.

Glancing round, the four cousins saw a scene of panic all around them! Some of the passengers had kept their heads, but a great many people were

shouting and screaming and running about in alarm – either hurt themselves, or worried about their companions on the train. Everything was in confusion!

Julian called up to the young Canadian, who was still perched on top of the carriage. 'Coming down, Peter?'

However, Peter crouched where he was for a moment, to untie Dick's lasso. 'A pity to leave this good rope behind!' he said, smiling. 'Here – catch!'

And he threw the children the lasso and got ready to jump down after it. 'It's not a very big drop,' he told them. 'I can land on my feet all right.'

He probably would have done, too – but just as he was landing, his right foot struck one of the stones on the railway-track and he fell heavily, twisting his ankle. He uttered a cry of pain and lay motionless on the ground, with his eyes closed. He seemed to be unconscious.

Anne ran to him, crying, 'Peter – oh, Peter, what's the matter?'

The Canadian did not reply. George too came and knelt down beside him. She shook him gently by the shoulder. 'Wake up, Peter – wake up!' she said. 'Are you hurt?'

Peter opened his eyes, and tried to smile, but not very successfully. 'Yes – I – I think I've broken a leg!' he gasped.

It was actually his ankle he had broken, as the doctors were to find out when they X-rayed it later.

The horrified children saw the ankle swell up and turn blue before their very eyes.

'Perhaps it's only a sprain?' said Anne, hopefully.

But Peter could not help crying out with pain when his new friends took off his shoe and turned up his trouser-leg, even though they were being as gentle as they possibly could.

'We must get you to a doctor, or a hospital!' said Dick. 'Somebody must have raised the alarm by now – I don't suppose it'll be long before help comes.'

The sun was still quite warm, although it was evening, and it was rather too hot for comfort out in the open beside the derailed train, so the children carried Peter very carefully over to the shade of some bushes. Then they looked around them, wondering what to do next. Timmy came and licked Peter's face and then sat down beside him, as if to keep watch over him.

People were still scurrying about. There were some who knew first-aid and were walking up and down the track, giving helpful advice, but others were in a panic and didn't seem to have any idea what to do. A railwayman in his uniform stopped beside the children.

'You all right, kids?' he asked. 'Oh dear – got somebody hurt here, have you? Well, if you just wait a little while there'll be an ambulance coming soon. They've been told at the next station along the line. How about lending me a hand while you wait?'

Anne and Timmy stayed to keep Peter company, and Julian, Dick and George set to work. They helped lead bruised or frightened children away from the track, they rescued luggage from the overturned carriages where possible, and made themselves useful in all sorts of ways.

Help soon came. Several ambulances drove up, and Peter was taken to the nearest station. The Five went with him. A local doctor was looking after those passengers who had been hurt, deciding if they needed to go to hospital.

The stationmaster, who seemed to be a very sensible person, asked any passengers who lived nearby to get their families to come and pick them up, and said there would soon be coaches to take other people on their way. George asked if she could ring her parents up. It was Aunt Fanny who answered the phone.

'We're all right, Mother,' George assured her at once. 'So don't worry! But do you think Father could come and collect us in the car?'

'He's on his way at this very moment,' said Aunt Fanny. 'News of the accident reached Kirrin a little while ago, and I was quite sick with worry! Oh, thank goodness you rang! I wanted to go with your father, but he wouldn't let me in case you'd come to any harm. So just wait a little while, and he'll be there to bring you home.'

Sure enough, Uncle Quentin soon turned up. The children would hardly have known him!

Usually he was so stern and reserved – but today anyone could see he was terribly upset, and he was quite pale with anxiety. He was so relieved to find George and her cousins safe and sound that he hugged them all.

'We've got a friend here too, Father,' George told him. 'He's hurt his ankle. It's Peter Darcy – the grandson of old Mr Darcy who used to live at Fairfields.'

'He's awfully nice, Uncle Quentin,' said Dick. 'We got to know him on the train.'

Uncle Quentin followed the children into the station waiting-room. Mattresses had been laid on the floor to take the injured passengers, and Peter Darcy was lying motionless on one of them, looking very pale. A doctor was leaning over him examining his ankle. Poor Peter had to bite his lip to keep from crying out with pain.

'Are you a relation of this young man?' the doctor asked Uncle Quentin, straightening up.

'No, but I knew his grandfather,' said Uncle Quentin.

'Peter comes from Canada,' Anne explained. 'He hasn't got any family in England at all.'

'We must look after him, Father!' cried George. 'We simply *must*!'

A smile lit up Uncle Quentin's rather severe face. 'What exactly is the matter with him?' he asked the doctor.

'He's broken his right ankle. We'll get him into a hospital bed somewhere as soon as we can.'

The doctor went off to see to some of the other injured passengers, and Uncle Quentin turned to Peter Darcy and introduced himself. 'How about coming to Kirrin Cottage Hospital?' he suggested. 'It's not a very big place, but very well equipped and efficient – and Dr Moore, a friend of mine, runs it, so I know I can get you in there. I've an idea my daughter and her friends will be wanting to visit you, and they could do that more easily if you're in Kirrin and not a big city hospital somewhere! What do you say?'

Peter managed to smile. 'I say thank you very much, sir! If I have to be in hospital, I'd sooner it was in Kirrin than anywhere else! Did you say you knew my grandfather?'

'Yes, I did. Edmund Darcy used to take an interest in my research – I'm a scientist, you know. We didn't often discuss personal subjects, but he did mention you to me. Ah, here come some more ambulances, so now let's see about getting you into the Cottage Hospital!'

Next day Peter Darcy, with his ankle in plaster, was just finishing his breakfast when the Five burst into his room – or rather the Four, because they had not been allowed to bring Timmy into the hospital with them! Like all the rooms in Kirrin Cottage Hospital, Peter's was bright and sunny. It was on the ground floor, with a window looking out on a pretty flower garden.

'Hallo, Peter!' said Anne. She had brought the invalid a bunch of roses from Aunt Fanny's garden. 'I hope you slept all right?'

'Is your ankle feeling any better?' asked Dick.

Anne arranged the roses in a vase, and Julian and George asked Peter how he was, too. Aunt Fanny had made some delicious little sponge cakes that morning, and George had brought some with her for their new friend. 'They'll help you to keep your strength up!' she told him.

'Woof!' Timmy agreed.

The five of them looked at the open window in surprise. There was Timmy, with his front paws up on the window-sill! His eyes were bright with mischief! Anyone could see he was very pleased with himself for the clever way he had got round the hospital regulations. If he wasn't allowed inside, then he was going to come in through the garden!

Everyone laughed! 'What a clever old thing you are, Timmy!' his little mistress told him, lovingly. 'You know, whenever we have adventures Timmy always joins in, Peter. And we've had some *very* exciting adventures in our time!'

'Have you really?' said Peter. 'You didn't tell me that before – let's hear about them!'

So Dick started to tell him about some of the thrilling times the Five had had. Peter seemed quite surprised to hear how often they'd managed to solve difficult problems which even baffled the police – but he believed every word they said.

Dick was just a little bit boastful about it, and when he had finished, Julian said, 'My brother isn't exactly famous for his modesty! But it's true that we *have* had some good luck – and if ever *you* have a problem to be solved, Peter, just call on us! Meanwhile, here's something for you to read. I brought you the daily papers. Look – you're in the news!'

'Me?' asked Peter, in surprise.

'Yes – at least, your name's on the list of people injured in the train accident. There's a full report in the local paper here.'

Peter leafed through the sheets of newspaper rather absent-mindedly. He seemed to be thinking of something else, and all of a sudden he said, 'Listen – I do believe it's Fate that brought us together! I liked you young people as soon as I met you – I even seem to have told you most of my life story, and I don't often do *that* with anyone, particularly strangers . . .'

He stopped, looking thoughtful. George guessed he was on the brink of telling them something else. She had a mysterious sixth sense which told her when there was some kind of adventure coming the Five's way – and that sixth sense was on the alert now.

'Go on!' she said encouragingly.

'Well,' said Peter, 'since I was prepared to trust you yesterday, I don't see why I shouldn't tell you a bit more today – especially as you tell me you like solving mysterious problems!'

Four pairs of interested and shining eyes were turned on him.

'Woof!' said Timmy, at the window. 'Woof, woof, *woof*!'

Peter smiled. 'And since Timmy obviously thinks it would be a good idea too, I'll tell you the whole story – my big secret, though I've never breathed a word to anyone before. Come closer, would you? I don't want to speak too loud, just in case someone overhears us. Well, this is how it was . . .'

Chapter Three

A MYSTERIOUS PICTURE

'After my grandfather's funeral,' Peter Darcy told the children, 'I had a letter from his lawyer. I had not been over to England for the funeral myself, because Grandfather particularly said he didn't want me to come – he knew I had important exams, and even when he was dying he didn't let me know how ill he was. However, he had written me a short note which the lawyer sent on to me, together with a sealed envelope. Grandfather's letter said something like this: "This envelope contains the key to my fortune! No one else knows anything about it. Make good use of your wealth, my boy. You could use it to set up a research centre, or a special clinic, or something of that kind, once you've qualified as a doctor." '

The Canadian paused. The four children were fascinated by his story, and never took their eyes off him. After a moment or so he went on.

'Well, when I read that note I thought there really *must* be a lot of money concerned. Grandfather was a very cautious man, and he made sure his investments were in things that would always hold their value, like gold and precious stones. So I thought that by "key" he meant a real one, and I'd find the key to a safe or a strong-box inside the envelope. However, he must have meant "clue", because when I opened the envelope, this was all it contained.'

As he spoke, Peter brought out a handsome blue leather wallet which he had had tucked under his pillow. He opened it.

'I always keep the envelope on me,' he explained, 'just to be on the safe side!'

He took a yellow envelope made of heavy, good quality paper out of the wallet. It had been sealed with wax, and the wax was broken.

'There – take a look at it for yourselves!' he told the children.

George took the envelope, opened it, and brought out a thick sheet of paper folded in four. She unfolded the paper and looked at it with surprise. It was a picture in pen and ink. Several different colours of ink had been used, and the picture showed a gentleman in old-fashioned but very fine clothes.

Julian, Dick and Anne all uttered exclamations of surprise too.

'A portrait!' said Anne.

'But what does it mean?' asked Julian.

'It doesn't look all *that* valuable!' Dick remarked.

Peter was able to tell them rather more about the portrait — but it still didn't shed much light on what his grandfather had meant!

'It's a reproduction of a picture which hangs in my grandfather's bedroom, but much smaller than the original, and done in ink. I remember how he once showed me the picture and told me it was a portrait of one of our ancestors, Sir Piers Darcy, who was one of King Charles II's courtiers.'

'Perhaps the portrait itself is valuable,' said Dick, puzzled, 'but I don't see that this sketch can really be worth a lot!'

'I really don't know!' sighed Peter. 'And I keep wondering . . . actually, the genuine portrait isn't of any great value either, I know that much. And another thing is that Grandfather always loved riddles and secrets! He was a bit of an eccentric. I wouldn't be at all surprised if there was some hidden meaning in that picture!'

'Woof!' agreed Timmy, very wisely. He seemed to be following every word of the conversation.

'Yes,' said George. 'I'm sure you're right, Peter. There must be some secret in it, or why did your grandfather send it to you?'

But at this point a nurse came in and interrupted the conversation. It was time for the children to leave — but they promised Peter to come back at visiting time that evening.

They felt very sorry for poor Peter in his hospital bed as they played about in the garden and on the beach, and they were back at the Cottage Hospital to cheer him up as soon as they were allowed in that evening.

'I say, Peter,' Julian told him, 'we've been thinking about you and your problem, and we all agree that your drawing there *must* be the sort of "key" that's a clue. Perhaps it really *does* tell you where to find a safe or something like that, just as you thought when you first opened the envelope.'

'He means there could be a clue to it in the picture somewhere,' Dick explained. 'And that's the key to the secret.'

'Speaking of keys,' said Peter, searching his wallet again, 'why don't I give you the keys to Fairfields? Then you could go and have a look round the house! Grandfather's bedroom is on the first floor, and if you go into it you can see the original portrait of Sir Piers. I don't know if that will tell you any more than we already know, but it's always possible.'

'What a shame you can't come with us!' said tender-hearted Anne.

'You're telling me it is!' said Peter, making a face. 'Not that it isn't very comfortable in this hospital – but I hate being stuck here with a foot in plaster at a time like this!'

'You'll just have to hurry up and get better,' George told him. 'And meanwhile you can rely on us to do all we can to solve your mystery – can't he, Timmy dear!'

'Woof!' barked Timmy.

He had been nowhere in sight – but now, to Peter's surprise, his big, hairy head popped out of a huge basket which Dick and George were carrying between them!

'You see, we're the Five,' George explained, perfectly seriously, 'and we simply *hate* to be separated!'

The cousins were feeling rather excited when they went back to Kirrin Cottage that evening. It was fun to have a new adventure on their hands! After supper they went out into the garden. The sun was sinking among beautiful golden and crimson clouds, and they watched it set as they decided on their plan of action.

'The first thing to do is go and look at Fairfields!' Julian said. 'We'll do that tomorrow morning. With any luck we might find another clue somewhere there.'

So next morning they set off. The property old Mr Darcy had left his grandson was a very handsome Elizabethan house. It was in good repair, and the big garden all round it had obviously been well tended too until quite recently – but weeds had sprung up all over the pathways and flower-beds in the two months since the old gentleman's death. Peter was going to have to find a gardener soon, unless he was very fond of gardening himself!

The Five went through the garden gate, walked along a gravel path, and climbed some steps up to the front door of the house. There were two sets of keys to let them in. The electricity had been turned off, but Dick soon found the mains switch in the fuse cupboard, with the aid of his torch, and he turned it on again. Now they could switch on the lights in all the rooms – not that they needed to do that except in one rather dark little pantry, because sunlight came flooding in through the windows.

'Now then – let's get down to work!' said George. 'We'll open a few windows to air the ground floor here, and then go up to visit Sir Piers on the first floor!'

Before the Five went upstairs, they had a quick look in the downstairs rooms – the drawing room, the dining room, the library, and old Mr Darcy's study. They soon realised that the whole house was full of precious things! Two glass cases in the library contained pieces of old jewellery and some lovely golden plates.

Once the children got up to the first floor, they easily found the old gentleman's bedroom. And there was the portrait of Sir Piers hanging on the wall, smiling at them from its gilt frame!

Anne put on an 'old-world' sort of voice and said, 'Good morrow, gentle sir!' as she swept a deep curtsey.

Dick wasn't feeling so polite! 'You can wipe that silly smile off your face and tell us what you're hiding,' he told the portrait.

The first thing that occurred to the children, of course, was to take the picture off the wall and see if there was some kind of hiding place behind it. But the wall behind the canvas was perfectly blank. It didn't even sound hollow as they tapped it! Dick and Anne, disappointed, hung it back in place.

Julian and George were searching the far corners of the room, with the help of Timmy, his nose close to the ground.

'What are you looking for?' asked Dick, puzzled.

'A strong-box, of course!' said his cousin. 'We didn't see anything of the kind downstairs – and I don't see one up here, either. That's funny.'

'Yes, it is,' agreed Julian. 'You'd have thought someone with as many treasures in his house as old Mr Darcy would have a safe or strong-box to put the most precious ones in!'

'Yes,' said Dick. 'And do you remember – Peter told us that his grandfather's safe at the bank turned out to have nothing but papers about stocks and shares in it, although he said Mr Darcy liked to invest a lot of his money in gold and precious stones?'

'No gold at the bank, and no strong-box here!' said George, disappointed. Then she went back to the portrait and stood in front of it. 'I can only think that Sir Piers here knows more than we do!' she said. 'What a pity he doesn't seem to want to tell us!'

'Let's have a closer look at the picture,' Dick suggested.

But even a closer look told them no more. There didn't seem to be anything at all unusual about it, and the frame was made of solid wood, without any

possible hiding place for a secret catch. Timmy came to have a sniff at it, got his nose full of dust, and sneezed.

'A-tishoof!' he went, disgusted.

'He means it's no go!' George translated for the others, hanging the picture back in place again. 'Oh, well, we must look somewhere else!'

But once the picture was hanging on the wall she stood looking at it, frowning. Then she went closer, examined it again, stepped back, then forward, put her head on one side – all this time her cousins were watching her in silence. They didn't want to disturb her. Anyone could see she had an idea of some kind in her head – and George's ideas were often quite bright ones!

'That's funny,' she said at last, in an absent sort of way.

'What's funny?' Anne asked.

'His head – or rather his long, curly wig!'

'What's the matter with his wig?' asked Julian, squinting at it. *He* couldn't see anything odd about it. 'I mean, we'd looked pretty silly wearing wigs like that now, but they were in fashion in the time of King Charles II!'

'Yes, but it's not exactly like the wig in the drawing Peter showed us. You know I've got a good visual memory, and –'

'Hang on,' Dick interrupted. 'You really mean the wig in the drawing isn't like the wig in this picture!'

George looked at her cousin. 'Yes, you're right,

Dick. Well done! That's the right way round – the wig in the drawing isn't like the one in the original.'

'Meaning exactly what?' asked Julian, who still couldn't make out what his cousin was getting at.

'Meaning that if there's a *difference* between the copy and the original, that difference may be the key to the mystery.'

'But how can we find out what –' Anne began.

'By comparing them, of course! Quick – we must go and ask Peter to lend us his drawing!'

They were in time for morning visiting hours at the hospital, and they told Peter what they had found at Fairfields – or rather, what they hadn't found! He seemed to be very interested in what George had to tell him about her theory of the difference between the portrait and the drawing.

'Are you sure they're not the same?' he asked.

'Almost – but I want to compare them, and that would mean borrowing your drawing. We'd take *very* good care of it!'

Peter hardly hesitated for a moment. He had liked the Five from the moment they met, and he trusted them all the more now he knew them better. 'Here you are!' he said, taking the yellow envelope out of his wallet. 'There's the drawing!'

He unfolded it again. All four cousins leaned eagerly over it. At first they couldn't see anything unusual about it, but then they noticed that the long, curly wig Sir Piers was wearing had rather odd marks in it at places.

'George, you're right!' Julian exclaimed. 'There

is something funny about the wig in this drawing!'

'It's as if there were little bits of wire in it, making it all stiff!' said Anne.

'Yes, so it is,' Peter agreed. 'That's because of the way the artist was drawing it, with lots of little straight lines. Look, there are hardly any curves here, even among the curls of the wig.'

'Wait a minute!' cried Dick, searching his pockets – quite a task, because they were full of odds and ends! 'Here's my magnifying glass! Now we can take a closer look!'

George was so impatient to have her theory confirmed that she practically snatched the magnifying glass from Dick, and put it to her own eye. She studied the intricate mass of little lines making up Sir Piers's wig for some time – and then, suddenly, she let out a cry of triumph.

'Hooray! I think I've got it! Look – look at that, all of you! There are tiny little letters and numbers hidden in his hair – they run all along the locks of the wig and they're all mixed up in its different colours!'

Chapter Four

THE SECRET OF THE WIG

The children passed the magnifying glass round from one to another. George was right! If they looked through the glass they really could see letters and figures, written in very thin, tiny strokes of the pen, and hidden among the drawing of the rest of the curly wig. What a clever idea!

'It's a message!' cried Dick. He was very excited. 'So *that's* the secret good old Sir Piers was hiding! We don't even need to go back to Fairfields to compare this drawing with the original portrait now!'

'But if it's a message, it's a very difficult one to read,' Anne pointed out.

'Yes, the tiny letters seem all muddled up,' Julian agreed with his little sister.

'Never mind!' said Peter Darcy. He was beaming. 'I knew I was right to trust you to solve the problem! You've done wonderfully well already –

I'm sure you'll manage to decipher the message too. My grandfather obviously left it on purpose for me!'

Julian had picked up the magnifying glass again. He was looking very closely at the little letters and figures.

'Look, I think there's a kind of guideline here,' he told the others. 'The figures and letters follow in line along alternate curls of the wig. The general impression you get is that it's a black wig, but there are chestnut and reddish and even slightly purple lights in it. It's drawn in several different colours of ink. Suppose each colour-change means a different sentence?'

'But it's all so tiny we can't really read the letters properly,' said Anne.

'Anne's right,' George agreed. 'Still, there's nothing to stop us making an enlargement of it – then we could trace several copies, sticking to the same colours as before, of course, and see if there really *is* any special meaning in the colours, as Julian suggests.'

'Well, take the drawing home with you and do just as you like,' said Peter. 'I'm in your hands – and very good hands they seem to be.'

'Dick's the best of us at art,' said Julian. 'He'll have to do most of the work. Hard luck, old chap!' he told his brother. 'Didn't know you were going to be put to work even in the holidays, did you?'

'Oh, I don't mind!' said Dick, grinning. 'Art lessons at school aren't like *real* work.' He really

42

was good at drawing, and always enjoyed it.

'I've got plenty of paper and pencils at home, in all the colours we need,' said George. 'So come on, everyone! We don't want to waste any more time.' She turned to Peter Darcy again. 'We'll bring you back your picture this evening, Peter. By then we'll each of us have a traced copy of it! See you soon!'

When they came out of the hospital they found that the bright sunlight of the early morning had disappeared. The sky was clouding over, and soon it began to rain – a steady drizzle which showed no sign of stopping.

'Never mind,' said Julian. 'We were going to spend the afternoon trying to decipher that message anyway, so it doesn't matter so much if we can't go bathing or cycling as usual.'

Timmy decided that he'd have an afternoon nap for once, and after dinner the children settled down round the table in the boys' room. They set to work, and soon each of them had a set of five tracings taken from Peter's picture. That had been Dick's idea: he thought of tracing the whole picture first, and then the separate details of the wig, with different tracings for the black, chestnut, red and purple hair. It was a lot of work, but it did make things clearer. The children pored over the mysterious marks on the tracings, and whenever they thought they'd deciphered a word or a number they wrote it down on a separate sheet of plain white paper.

George and her cousins worked hard, pooling all

their results, and after a while they had the whole message written down.

The only trouble was, it didn't seem to make sense!

The letters and figures written in the black part of the wig read:

CRETE 2   DING 4   SEA 1   PLAICE 5   HIE 3

Those written in the chestnut-brown locks said:

YOU 2   SAID 3   TURN 5   DIS 1   SIS 4

The reddish part of the message seemed to say:

RITE 3   STOW 1   NON 2   STOP 342

And finally, the bits in purple ink said:

JUST 3   BEE 1   WEAR 2   IN 4

'But it's simply nonsense!' said Anne, shaking her head in disappointment.

'No – I don't think it *is* nonsense!' cried George. She was suddenly feeling very excited. 'I think it's going to be quite easy to crack the code of this message!'

She bent over the paper where she had written everything down, and explained what she meant.

'Suppose each separate colour does contain one sentence or phrase, as Julian thought at first! And then suppose the numbers tell you the order of the words in the sentence!'

'Hang on!' said Dick. 'That would mean that 342 after the word STOP said STOP was the three hundred and forty-second word in its sentence, and you can see there aren't anything like that number of words in the whole message!'

'Well, let's just try with the rest of the words,'

said George.

The children set to work again, and when they had written out the words in the order given by the numbers after them, this was the result:

SEA CRETE HIE DING PLAICE
DIS YOU SAID SIS TURN
STOW NON RITE STOP 342
BEE WEAR JUST IN

It *still* didn't seem to make sense!

They all stared at the message in silence for a few moments – and then Dick and George shouted, both at once, 'Got it!'

'Got what?' asked Anne.

'It's easy!' said George, scribbling away on her piece of paper. 'The words are spelt wrong on purpose! All you have to do is put the spelling right, and *then* you get a message saying, "Secret hiding place – disused cistern – stone on right – stop 342 – beware . . . just in?" ' She was chewing the end of her pencil and shaking her head. 'That last bit is the part I still don't understand. I suppose the word "stop" is there to keep the rest of the sentence separate from the number, 342. But it's hard to see what the number is there *for*. Oh well, I suppose we'll find out later.'

'Yes – the main thing is that now we know there *is* a secret hiding place,' said Julian. 'And we have to look for a disused cistern of some kind, and a stone that's important in some way – at least, that's how I understand the message.'

'I expect the hiding place is somewhere in the

house or garden at Fairfields,' said Anne.

'Hold on!' said Dick. 'We haven't worked out what the end of the message means yet – in fact it doesn't seem to *have* a proper end at all! Beware of – but then we've got "just in", and nothing after that!'

'Yes, I'm stuck on the words "just in" myself,' George admitted.

'Wait a minute!' said Julian. 'Suppose it's all one word – JUSTIN? A first name! It could be the name of somebody old Mr Darcy didn't trust, and he wanted to warn Peter!'

George jumped to her feet. 'Come on, it's nearly visiting hours at the hospital! Let's go and see Peter. He may be able to throw some light on the message – and won't he be pleased to know we really *have* found the "key" to the secret of his legacy!'

The noise the children made as they pushed their chairs back woke Timmy up, and he jumped up too, wagging his tail. He knew something was going to happen – and whatever it was, dear old Timmy wasn't going to be left out of it!

Peter Darcy was delighted when the children told him about the message they had found hidden in the curls of Sir Piers's wig. If only his ankle hadn't been in plaster he'd have danced for joy! They were all talking so excitedly, and making so much noise, that a nurse opened the door of Peter's room and looked inside to see what was going on. Timmy had been smuggled in hidden in his basket again, and he only just had time to hide under the bed.

'Not so much noise in here, please!' said the nurse. 'Or I'll have to forbid you children to visit my patient in future.'

The children said they were sorry, and once the nurse had gone away again they went back to discussing the difficult part of the message – but more quietly this time.

'The bit we don't understand is that number, 342, and the name Justin,' said George.

Peter's face darkened suddenly. 'The number doesn't mean anything to me either,' he said, 'but the name Justin certainly does! Oh, I wish to goodness I wasn't stuck here in hospital! As soon as I'm up and about again I'll be able to join in your hunt – if you haven't got any farther with it by then. But as for Justin –'

'Go on,' said George, as Peter hesitated. 'Who *is* this Justin?'

'I'm afraid he's rather a bad lot. I don't like to talk about him, because the fact is, he's a distant relation of our family, though only by marriage. A sort of second cousin. Grandfather told me that he once had Justin to stay here in Kirrin, when he hadn't anywhere else to go – but so far from being grateful, Justin tried to steal some of Grandfather's valuable pieces of jewellery. So of course Grandfather sent him packing – and ever after that he was afraid Justin might come back. He thought he was more dangerous than an ordinary thief would be, because he knew about all the precious things Grandfather had collected.'

'What does this Justin look like?' asked Anne.

'Well, he's at least fifteen years older than me, and so he was grown up the only time I ever met him, when I came to England for a short visit as a child. I remember him as being short, thin and very dark. But that's a long time ago. He could have got thinner or gone grey-haired by now.'

'All the same, he won't have grown any taller,' said Dick. 'Not if he was grown up when you met him. So that means a short man, who might well have stayed thin – at least we have *some* kind of a clue there.'

'Let's just hope he doesn't turn up – then there'll be no need to identify him!' said Peter. 'But we mustn't forget that he knows a lot about my grandfather's fortune.'

'Well, even if he suspects there *is* treasure hidden at Fairfields, how would he set about looking for it?' said George cheerfully. 'Your grandfather didn't send *him* a picture of Sir Piers with clues in it – at least I don't suppose so, after what you've told us about him and this cousin Justin of yours!'

'No, you're quite right!' said Peter, laughing. 'Now, tell me – when are you going to start out on your treasure hunt?'

'I'm afraid we won't be able to begin searching till tomorrow afternoon,' said George, regretfully. 'It's too late to start today, and tomorrow morning we've got to do some shopping for Mother. You see, Father's going to London for one of his important scientific meetings, and he wanted Mother to go with him – so she's asked dear old Joan to come up from the village and stay in the house, but she doesn't want Joan to have *too* much work to do, so we said we'd do the shopping for her, and now I suppose we can't really get out of it!'

'Never mind,' said Peter. 'I think it's very nice of you to go treasure-hunting on my behalf at all – *and* to go shopping for Joan!'

'We'll look in and say good morning in visiting hours tomorrow, on our way back from the village,' Julian promised.

'Good,' said Peter, 'I'll look forward to that. See you tomorrow, then!'

Chapter Five

TREASURE-HUNTING AT FAIRFIELDS

George and her cousins did just as they had promised Peter they would. Aunt Fanny had given them a list of all the things they were to buy for Joan, and the next morning, when Aunt Fanny and Uncle Quentin had left for London, they went down to the village to do the shopping. On their way home they stopped at the hospital. They left their bicycles in the forecourt – and this time they left Timmy there too, to guard the shopping bags. The good dog would rather have gone in to see Peter with them, but he knew it was his duty to stay put when George told him to.

'Hallo, old chap!' said Dick cheerfully, as they entered Peter's room. But they all stopped short when they saw how worried their Canadian friend was looking.

'Oh dear – is your ankle worse, or something?' asked Julian.

'No, it's quite a bit better, but thanks for asking! However, I have some bad news for you – I was burgled last night!'

'Burgled?' said George. 'What happened? What did the burglar take?'

'Well – you know I always keep my window open, because I like the fresh air, and of course this room is on the ground floor. It looks as if somebody got in through the window while I was asleep. And whoever it was must have managed to feel under my pillow without waking me, because the nurse found my wallet on the floor this morning. My money and passport were still in it – but the yellow envelope containing the drawing of the wig had gone!'

'Oh dear!' said Dick. 'I suppose you think your burglar was Justin? And now he knows as much as we do!'

'We can't be sure of that,' said George. 'He hasn't got the tracings we did, or the complete message all worked out, so we've still got a good start on him.'

'And he may never manage to crack the code of the message at all!' said Anne.

Peter looked a little more cheerful. 'All the same, however did Justin find out where I was?' he murmured.

'He may have been in this part of the country ever since your grandfather's death,' suggested George. 'If he knew Fairfields was standing empty, he could have been waiting for a good opportunity to break in. And then your name's been in the papers. It was on the list of accident victims the day after the train was derailed.'

'Yes,' Anne agreed, 'and everybody would know that any of the accident victims who weren't taken to hospital in the nearest big town would be in the Cottage Hospital here in Kirrin!'

Peter was still very upset. The more he thought about it, the more sure he felt that Justin was the burglar who had broken into his room. His things had been searched, but nothing was taken except the picture in the yellow envelope. And his distant cousin Justin knew all about Edmund Darcy's eccentricity, and the old man's liking for puzzles and secrecy. However, he was not sure that the burglar had really been after the picture of Sir Piers when he broke in.

'I guess his real reason for coming would have been to steal the keys to Fairfields,' Peter told the children. 'What luck I gave them to you! But maybe, while he was looking for them in my wallet, he found the drawing and went off with it instead. Now he'll be nosing around Fairfields! We must stop him – I just wish to goodness I was on my feet again. There's no time to lose!'

'What a pity Uncle Quentin left for London first thing this morning!' said Julian. 'If he was here we could have told him, and then he'd have come to Fairfields with us – or maybe he'd have said the best thing was to go to the police. Would you like *us* to go and tell the police, Peter?'

Julian was a very sensible, responsible boy – sometimes a bit *too* sensible for his cousin George's liking!

'No, I don't think so,' said Peter Darcy, frowning. 'For a start, that would mean telling them my secret, and I'm not very keen to do that. And it would mean wasting precious time, too – that is, if you really can go and start searching this afternoon! What's more, they might not take our fears seriously at all, and then they just wouldn't bother to do anything.'

'You're right,' said Dick, and the others nodded. The Five had quite a lot of experience of not being taken seriously by the police! 'We'll go to Fairfields the moment we've had our dinner!'

'And if Justin's there we'll jolly well chase him away!' said Anne firmly, in her soft little voice.

That made Peter realise that his young friends could be in real danger if they went to Fairfields, and it would be his fault. He went red in the face, feeling rather ashamed of himself for not thinking of that before.

'Listen, all things considered, I think I'd rather you *didn't* go to Fairfields at all,' he said. 'You're only children – and supposing Justin's realised there's a treasure, and he's determined to get hold of it, he's quite capable of hurting you in some way. That's the very last thing I want!'

'You must be joking!' said Dick. 'We may be "only children", but I can tell you the five of us are as good as two grown-ups any day!'

'Timmy's as good as a grown-up all by himself!' said George proudly. 'If it comes to a fight or anything like that, *he* won't be caught on the hop, let me tell you!'

The idea of Timmy hopping about on one paw was so comical that Peter couldn't help laughing. Julian, Dick and Anne joined in too. George felt a little bit offended at first, and then she started to laugh as well!

Julian was the first to sober down again. 'Ssh!' he warned the others. 'We'll have that nurse coming down on us like a ton of bricks if we're not careful! Don't worry, Peter. We'll be quite all right – I shall make sure the others aren't in any danger.' The others looked a bit annoyed at this, but they knew Julian, as the eldest, meant well. 'And I wouldn't expect Justin to risk breaking into Fairfields before he's deciphered your grand-father's message. So what we have to do is get to the treasure before him, and put it in safe keeping somewhere.'

In the end, Peter let Julian have his way. He could see that the boy was trustworthy, so he agreed to let the Five carry out their original plan.

'But you must be very careful indeed,' he said. 'I'd never forgive myself if anything happened to you.'

'We'll make sure the house is empty before we go in,' Anne promised – though nobody knew just how she thought they could do that *without* going in to find out!

'And we'll leave Timmy on guard while we look for the cistern,' said George. 'Good old Timmy is the best watchdog in the world! Goodbye, Peter. We'll be back as soon as we have any news.'

Old Joan had brought a lovely fresh lettuce up from her own garden, and the children had bought cold ham and fresh rolls in Kirrin village, so they had a delicious salad for dinner. As soon as they had helped Joan clear away, they set off for Fairfields on their bicycles. Timmy always enjoyed a bit of exercise, and he ran happily along beside George's bike – chasing off the road now and then just to see if by any chance there were rabbits about.

When the Five got to Fairfields, they saw that the garden gate was locked, just as they had left it after their previous visit. Timmy led them to the house, going up the garden path ahead of them with his tail wagging. George was sure he wouldn't have been acting like that if he'd scented a stranger about the place anywhere. She told the others she thought it would be quite safe to go in.

Nobody seemed to have interfered with the lock on the front door either. The children unlocked it with both keys. They made sure that the house *was* empty and then came out again.

'Right!' said Dick. 'Now to find the secret hiding place in the disused cistern!'

The Five hadn't seen any sign of a disused cistern in the house, so they felt sure that old Mr Darcy's message meant they would have to search the garden for his hiding place. And the garden, as they knew already, was a really big one. It surrounded Fairfields on all sides, so each of the children set off to explore on one of the four sides of the house.

With the work divided up like this, it didn't take them long – and the results were disappointing.

'Not a cistern in sight!' said George, who was the first to arrive back at the house.

'I didn't find anything at all except a green-house,' Anne told her cousin.

And when the boys got back, they hadn't had any luck either.

'Oh, bother!' said Dick, crossly. 'It's not as if you could overlook a disused cistern! I mean, a cistern has to be quite large, to hold water – and the only one inside the house is quite a modern one and *does* hold water! We've already looked at it, up under the roof.'

'I wonder if there's another cistern up *on* the roof?' suggested Julian. 'A disused one left there when they put a modern water cistern in?'

But when they stood back from the house they could easily see the whole roof, and there was nothing that could possibly be an old cistern on top of it. The children looked at each other, rather downcast.

'What about the cellar?' said Anne.

So the Five ran down the steps leading to the cellar of the old house. They had only taken a brief look here before, but now they searched the place thoroughly. Yet again they were in for a disappointment. No sign of a disused cistern anywhere!

'Oh dear. I suppose we might as well go home to tea,' said Julian, at last. 'Perhaps this is a very *little* cistern, hidden somewhere in the garden! Let's come back straight after tea and go over the garden again with a fine toothcomb.'

They all agreed to do that. Joan had been making scones, and smiled broadly when she saw the children gobble them all up for tea, with thick clotted cream and strawberry jam – at least all their searching had given them a good appetite! As soon as they had finished, they cycled back to Fairfields again. They didn't want to be empty-handed when they went to see Peter in hospital that evening – they really *must* find some clue to the whereabouts of the treasure, and what was more, they must find it before Justin did!

'Let's begin our second search of the garden, and this time we'll make sure we're as thorough as if we were looking for a single particular pebble on a shingly beach!' said Julian.

'Even a tiny cistern isn't going to be small enough to hide in a tuft of grass!' grumbled Dick.

'Well, it's got to be *somewhere*,' said George firmly.

This time they all searched together, instead of dividing the garden up into four as they had that morning. 'Someone might see something the others miss,' said George.

They still found nothing at all in the front garden. So then they went round to the side, where the greenhouse stood. It was a long, low greenhouse, with glass all the way down to the ground, and some of the panes of glass could be opened. The four cousins were busy searching a corner of the greenhouse which was full of big, empty flower-pots, a wheelbarrow and a number of garden tools, when Timmy, who had been sniffing about the floor, suddenly stood still in front of one of the greenhouse doors and started growling quietly.

George looked up.

'Ssh!' she told the others. 'Timmy's heard something!'

Then Timmy let out a yelp of anger, and threw himself at the door. At that moment the children looked through the greenhouse panes, which happened to be made of frosted glass on that side of the building, and saw a shadowy figure outside. It disappeared at once, as if by magic.

'Oh!' squealed Anne. 'There was somebody there!'

'Yes – somebody who's been keeping watch on us and what we're doing!' said Dick.

George dashed to the door and opened it, and Timmy bounded out, barking furiously.

Chapter Six

ENTER JUSTIN!

By the time the children caught up with Timmy, the dog had reached the wall which separated the garden of Fairfields from the garden of the big house next to it. He was still barking, and looking up, as if he wanted to tell the children that the intruder had got away over the wall.

'Well, if he really jumped that wall he must be pretty agile!' said Dick.

Julian was frowning as he worked out the meaning of the incident. 'Why should anyone want to spy on us unless he was hoping we'd discover something — discover it *for* him, because he'd already been looking for it himself? And looking for it in vain!'

'You mean the treasure?' said Anne. 'Do you think that was Justin, then?'

'It does seem likely,' said Julian. 'So that's one more good reason for us to hurry up and find the cistern. Where on earth can it be?'

The Five were in a desperate hurry now, and they went on searching frantically. But they were still out of luck. They even found a garden rake and scratched away at the soil here and there, at places where they thought it might possibly cover the top of a cistern. However, that was no use either. At last they gave up, feeling exhausted.

They hadn't got anywhere at all!

It was time to go to the hospital, and they felt very downcast as they entered Peter's room. He was waiting for them impatiently.

'You didn't find anything, did you?' he said at once.

'I'm afraid not,' said George, shaking her head. 'And not for want of searching, I can tell you!'

'I'm so sorry – it's all my fault!' said their Canadian friend. This wasn't the reaction the four cousins had expected at all, and they looked at him in surprise.

'Yes – you see, after you left this morning I searched my memory,' Peter told them, 'and I realised I'd never seen a cistern anywhere in the garden of Fairfields when I visited Grandfather as a boy. So perhaps the one he meant was the old cistern at the top of a tower in the little wood which lies behind the house itself! It's an old tower, and all that remains of a building which once stood there.'

'My word!' cried Dick. 'We *did* notice the little wood – it starts just beyond the vegetable plot at the very end of the garden behind the house! But we didn't realise it belonged to the grounds of Fairfields.'

'Well, we'll go back tomorrow,' said Julian firmly, 'and then we'll see if we can't track your legacy down somehow!'

Anne was just opening her mouth to tell Peter about the shadowy and suspicious figure the children had seen, but George realised what she was about to say and made faces at her, telling her to shut up. They didn't want to worry their friend unnecessarily.

They all said good night to Peter and went home to Kirrin Cottage. They were rather late for supper, and dear old Joan scolded them, but she gave them a good hot supper all the same. They went to bed quite early that night. Even Timmy was almost asleep on his feet.

The children were up so early next morning that Joan was very surprised. 'My goodness me!' she said. 'Are you ready for your breakfast so soon?'

They were! Joan cooked lots of bacon and eggs. and they ate plenty of toast and honey too. They felt they needed a good hearty breakfast before they went back to their search for treasure at Fairfields!

As soon as they reached the house they hurried to the little wood, and they soon spotted the old tower Peter Darcy had mentioned.

'I say, it looks rather dilapidated,' murmured George. 'I just hope it doesn't fall to bits while we're climbing up inside it!'

However, the staircase inside the tower seemed to be all right. Julian went up first, to make sure it was safe for the others. He felt responsible for them. He tested each step carefully before he put his full weight on it, and the rest of the Five followed him. At last they came out at the top of the tower.

'And there's the cistern!' shouted Dick triumphantly.

Full of curiosity, they all looked at it. It was a little, square construction made of stone and concrete, and it was open to the air. There must once have been a lid, but it had disappeared, and so had the metal lining inside. Probably rust had eaten the metal away.

'Secret hiding place, disused cistern,' recited Anne. 'Well, if this really *is* where old Mr Darcy hid his fortune, we still don't know how to get at it. *I* can't see anything inside the cistern at all!'

'Don't forget the last bit of the message,' Dick reminded her. 'Stone on right!'

'Hm,' said George. 'I wonder just what he meant by that? I suppose we might as well start from the way we're facing.'

When the children had reached the top of the staircase they had come out right in front of the cistern, and its squared stones were facing them.

'It might mean one of the stones in this part of the cistern,' suggested Julian, stepping forward. 'Anyway, there's no harm in trying!'

He put the flat of his hand against the top right-

65

hand stone and pushed, hard. The stone moved slowly inwards, and the children heard a click. Then a whole part of the side of the cistern turned, revealing a recess. There was something shining at the back of this recess – the front of a metal safe, with three shiny knobs on it.

'We've done it!' cried George. 'I *thought* the sides of this cistern looked awfully thick! That's so that they would take this hiding place!'

But now the question was how to open the safe?

'Stop, 342,' Anne remembered.

'Why, of course! That's the answer!' said George. Her cousins looked at her, puzzled, and she explained, 'Look – there are three knobs on the front of that safe, and we need to know the right combination of numbers to work the mechanism that opens it. Well, that's it! The numbers we want must be the numbers in the message from old Mr Darcy – 3, 4 and 2!'

As she spoke, George put out her hand and began turning the knobs. She turned the left-hand one round three notches, the middle one four notches, and the right-hand one two notches. Then she pulled the little door of the safe towards her – and it opened effortlessly, without needing any further key.

Feeling very excited, the children craned their necks to look inside, and as if to help them, the morning sun came out from behind a cloud and shone right into the interior of the safe. It was a dazzling sight! The top shelf of the safe contained a tray of diamonds, the shelf below it had a similar tray on it, but carrying emeralds, and all the rest of the safe was stuffed with gold ingots.

Blinking at the magnificent sight, George put her hand out and picked up a diamond. The jewel was sparkling brightly in the sun. Anne couldn't help exclaiming delightedly, 'It's just like fireworks!'

Dick leaned forward and picked up a gold ingot. 'I wouldn't mind having a whole house built of bricks like *this*!' he joked.

George, who was still holding the diamond, took the ingot from her cousin so as to have a closer look at it.

For the last few moments, Timmy had been watching a mouse that was scurrying about a corner of the tower. All of a sudden he lost interest in the little creature, pricked up his ears, and opened his mouth to bark.

Too late! He had been so busy watching the mouse that he hadn't noticed a man climbing the stairs in almost complete silence, and now the newcomer had reached the top.

The four cousins were rooted to the spot – they certainly hadn't expected to see anyone else here, and Timmy would usually have given them warning in plenty of time. As for the man, he stopped dead too, staring at the scene before him.

One glance was enough to tell the children that this must be Peter's distant cousin Justin! He was about the same height as Julian, very thin and wiry, and his hair had once been very black, but now it was beginning to go grey. He had bright black eyes under bushy eyebrows, and altogether there was a sly sort of look about him. So in spite of all the precautions the children had taken, they were face to face with their enemy – and at the worst possible moment, too! The very moment when they had just discovered old Mr Darcy's treasure!

What Justin saw – or thought he saw – was a party consisting of three boys in jeans, a little girl with pretty, fair hair, and a mongrel dog. He didn't think *they* would present many problems! He smiled, and Anne noticed that he had very yellow, rather pointed teeth. She had been thinking of him as the black sheep of Peter's family, but those teeth made him look more like a wolf.

She noticed something else, too. Justin was carrying a pistol!

He took a step forward, pointing his gun at the children.

'Right!' he snapped. 'You can put those ingots and precious stones in here for me!'

And he tossed an ordinary canvas bag at the children's feet.

'So my suspicions were correct!' he added, with a nasty, spiteful smile. 'I knew you'd lead me to old Darcy's hoard in the end!'

The Five still didn't budge. Timmy was only waiting for George to give the word, and he would have jumped at the man – but Justin had a gun, and George wasn't going to put her beloved dog in danger.

'Hurry up!' Justin said. 'Don't just stand there! Put that stuff in my bag, I tell you!'

Anne was breathing rather fast in her alarm. Julian and Dick exchanged glances as they tried to think what to do next. But for that gun, they, like Timmy, would have tackled the intruder by now.

George was the first person to do anything. She acted quickly and with decision! Before Justin realised what she was up to, she threw the diamond and the ingot she was holding back into the safe, closed the little armour-plated door, and rapidly turned all three knobs to mix up the combination that would open it again.

Justin stood watching her with his mouth open. 'Here – what d'you think you're doing, boy?' he stammered. Yet another person who thought George was a boy at first sight! 'I didn't tell you to shut the safe! I want all that stuff in my bag!'

The children could see that he was simply furious. First the blood rose to his face, then it ebbed away again, leaving him very pale. His voice rose, quivering with anger.

'Open up that safe or I fire!'

George thought fast. She felt sure he was quite capable of using the pistol to try intimidating them – and he might well hurt someone! They *had* to gain time somehow!

She gave her cousins a warning glance. Julian and Dick met her eyes. They knew how well

George's brain worked in an emergency – faster than theirs, quite often! – and they managed to let their cousin know, without any words, that whatever she did they'd back her up. As for Anne, she'd got her self-control back. The little girl had a sweet, quiet nature, and was rather timid in the usual way, but the others knew that she could be remarkably brave when they were facing real danger. George was sure she could count on Anne just as much as she could rely on the boys and good old Timmy.

Justin was still pointing his pistol at her.

'Now just you listen, my lad!' he said. 'I'm going to count to three. If you haven't opened up that safe by the time I've finished, I'll shoot you in the calf of your leg, understand? It won't be fatal, but by golly, it'll hurt! All right, here we go! One . . . '

George's brain was working away like lightning. She took in every detail of Justin's appearance – his little eyes, which were rather close together, his forehead, which was low and wrinkled and looked like a monkey's – no, she didn't think he looked particularly intelligent!

'In fact, he *can't* be very bright,' thought George, 'or he'd know better than to think he could carry so much gold away with him in an ordinary canvas bag! There must be a hundred ingots in the safe – they'd make a hole in his bag in no time, and even if they didn't I don't see that little man being able to carry such a heavy weight!'

'Two!' said Justin.

'What's more,' George added, to herself, 'he wanted me just to chuck the diamonds and emeralds in with the gold ingots! That really *was* a silly idea! The diamonds would have been all right — diamonds are very hard. But emeralds are different. They easily get cracks and flaws in them. Yes, our friend Justin is pretty stupid.'

'Th —' Justin began.

George raised one hand. She had decided that if Justin was as stupid as she suspected, it would be worth trying a bit of bluff, just to frighten him.

'Stop!' she said. 'There's something I'd better tell you. My cousins don't know the combination of the safe — I'm the only one who does, and I'm not giving it away to anyone. And if you fire that gun at me, my dog will get you by the throat long before you've had time to fire it at him too!'

George's boldness took her cousins' breath away — and Justin was staggered, too. He'd never expected these children to put up any resistance at all!

He hesitated, not sure what to do next, and his arm, holding the gun, trembled very slightly.

This was the moment Anne chose to come to her cousin's aid!

Chapter Seven

A TRIUMPH – AND A SHOCK

Pretending to be really terrified, Anne clutched at her heart and suddenly started to stagger about, babbling, 'Oh dear, oh dear – I feel so awful – oh, what shall I do?'

She had drawn Justin's attention to herself, just as she intended. He took his eyes off George for a moment – and with one leap, George grabbed him by the arm and was hanging on. He dropped his pistol. Both at once, Julian and Dick jumped on their enemy and tried to overpower him. As for Timmy, now that George gave him the word he was more than delighted to sink his teeth into Justin's leg!

Once Justin had got over his surprise he hit out in self-defence – and he was so angry it seemed to make him stronger than you would have expected from his small size. He was flailing his arms about like the sails of a windmill. One of his fists hit Dick on the shoulder and sent him flying. Shaking off George and Julian, who were still hanging on to him, he managed to catch them off balance, and he seized his chance to make a dash for the staircase. He gave Timmy a vicious kick, which knocked the breath right out of the poor dog for a moment, and made his escape.

It took the Five a few moments to gather their wits together again. By the time they set off in pursuit of Justin, he had reached the bottom of the tower.

Timmy galloped after him, barking furiously. He wanted his revenge! The four children ran down the stairs as fast as they could go.

The chase led them through the little wood. Justin crashed through bushes, swerved around trees, and did all he could to throw the children off his trail. But if he thought he could get away from Timmy he was being a lot too hopeful!

Just as the four cousins had lost sight of him, they suddenly heard him let out a cry of pain. 'Ouch!' And then they saw their quarry shoot out of a thicket – with Timmy firmly attached to the seat of his trousers!

It was such a funny sight that Julian, Dick, Anne and George all burst out laughing.

'*Good* dog, Timmy!' cried George. 'Hold tight, old boy!'

Seeing the children running towards him, Justin made one more desperate effort to shake Timmy off. This time he managed it, and he dashed off again – just like one of those rabbits Timmy loved to chase! But he forgot to look where he was going, stumbled over a tree root, and fell to the ground. He hit his head on a tree trunk as he fell and knocked himself unconscious!

The Five lost no time in dealing with him. These days, Dick and George carried their coiled lassoes everywhere with them, so that they could practise throwing whenever they got a spare moment – and their craze came in very useful now. They unhitched the coiled ropes from their belts, and tied Justin up, while Anne and Timmy watched. Meanwhile, Julian ran back to the tower to retrieve Justin's pistol and make sure the safe was properly shut.

When he came back, the children held a council of war.

'Justin's coming round, but he's still too groggy for us to make him walk to the police station,' said Dick. 'And if people saw him walking through Kirrin with his hands tied it would mean a lot of publicity. We know Peter doesn't want anything like that – after all, Justin *is* one of his family, even if he's only a distant relation.'

'You're right,' said George. 'We won't walk him through the village – we'll leave him here. He's well trussed up, and he won't be able to get away. We'll go to the police ourselves, and all we need tell them is that we found a trespasser on the Darcys' property!'

'Good idea!' said Anne approvingly. 'I'm sure

Peter would prefer that.'

'And we needn't mention Peter's fabulous legacy, either,' said Julian. 'Come along, then, everybody!'

The four children got on their cycles and rode off as fast as they could go. The Sergeant at Kirrin police station knew George and her cousins quite well. He listened to what the children had to say, and then decided to drive straight to Fairfields in a police car with one of his men. He was even kind enough to use a van which would take all the children as well, so that they could come too!

But there was a big disappointment in store for them. When they reached the spot where they had left their prisoner, there wasn't anybody there at all. Only the two lassoes were left, lying on the ground. Justin had disappeared.

'We can't have pulled the knots tight enough, and he managed to get free!' said Dick crossly.

George was simply furious with herself. She liked to think she always had her wits about her – but for once she'd been careless, and she knew it.

'I ought to have stayed to keep watch over him, with Timmy!' she said, fuming. 'Oh, how *stupid* of me! I bet he's miles away by now!'

The only proof they had that their 'trespasser' had ever existed at all was the pistol he had used to threaten them. Julian handed it over to the policemen. Then they all went off to visit Peter Darcy in hospital.

Peter was astonished when the Sergeant told

him that 'Miss Kirrin and her cousins had found a trespasser on his land'. But Dick winked hard at him behind the policemen's backs, so he realised that this was only a sort of 'official' version of the true story. So he agreed to lay official charges, though the policemen said they doubted if there was much chance of catching the supposed trespasser.

After the policemen had left, the children told their Canadian friend what had really happened, and all about their adventure. Peter hardly knew whether to be pleased or alarmed after the event!

'That's fantastic!' he cried. 'You're terrific kids! You actually found the safe and opened it! I owe you a lot for finding my legacy, I really do – but I hate to think of the risks you were running, confronting Justin like that. And you mustn't go back to Fairfields again. I don't want you to be in any more danger!'

'That's just too bad!' said George firmly. 'You asked us to solve your problem, didn't you, seeing you were in hospital and couldn't get about yourself? Well, we said we would, and now we're jolly well going to see our mission through to the end!'

'We *can't* just stay away from the house, you know,' said Julian. Even he agreed with George this time. 'Don't forget, Justin knows exactly where the treasure is, and I'm sure he's capable of breaking into the safe hidden in the cistern!'

'Well, the answer's simple, then!' said Peter,

making up his mind. 'I'll get in touch with the police again and tell them everything.'

'Oh no!' cried Dick. 'I'm sure it would be better if you don't do that – as soon as people know about that treasure you'll be simply plagued by all sorts of people – journalists, people begging from you –'

'And all that publicity would be bound to attract thieves!' Anne pointed out in her quiet little voice. 'Peter, you told us yourself to keep quiet about the treasure!'

'Well, the circumstances are different now!'

'Oh no, they're not!' George said firmly. 'Listen, all we have to do is get the treasure to safety. Then we won't be in any danger ourselves. I shouldn't think Justin will go straight back to the tower – he'll probably wait for night to fall before he tries anything else. And by that time we'll have moved your treasure out of the tower, Peter! When my father comes home, we'll tell him all about it, and he'll go to the bank and hire a bank vault for you. Then you won't have anything to worry about any more.'

In the end, the children talked Peter round.

'But *where* are you planning to hide the gold and jewels until Mr Kirrin comes back from London?' he asked.

'Oh, I've thought of that!' Julian told him. 'There's a little trailer which can be fastened on behind a bicycle in the garage at Kirrin Cottage. We'll use it to take the gold ingots home with us and bury them in the garden, under cover of dark.

77

They'll be quite safe there until Uncle Quentin comes back.'

'And I know what to do with the diamonds and emeralds!' said Anne. 'We can hide them in my doll's house. No burglar would ever think of looking for them there!'

Peter agreed to these plans, and the children decided that the best thing would be to carry them out at once.

'And it's just too bad if we're late for dinner!' said Dick bravely – he was making a great sacrifice, because Joan was a marvellous cook, and she had been going to make Dick's favourite toad-in-the-hole today!

Peter still felt a little bit worried as he said goodbye to his young friends. He was an active young man by nature, and he really hated being tied to a hospital bed while other people looked after his interests for him. It almost made him feel sorry he'd ever let the Five start off on their treasure hunt at all!

'Well, the sooner the contents of that safe are out of the tower the better,' he said to himself. 'At least those brave kids won't be in any more danger then!'

While Peter was brooding like this, wishing his ankle would hurry up and get better, the Five themselves were running back to Kirrin Cottage as fast as they could to fetch the little trailer. Then they picked up their bicycles, which they had left at the police station, and set off along the road to

Fairfields.

This time they kept looking back to make sure there wasn't anyone following them. They didn't trust Peter's distant cousin Justin a bit!

'Oh, good!' said Dick, looking back once more as they got off their cycles outside the garden gate of Fairfields. They had a good view of the road behind them, and there wasn't a soul in sight. 'Nobody's followed us here!'

He turned out to be quite right. Nobody *had* followed the Five to Fairfields.

But somebody had been there before them!

They reached the top of the tower only to find the safe open and the treasure gone! The thief had used some kind of explosive to blow the door open – it could have been simply the powder out of several gun cartridges. And the children had a very good idea of who the thief must have been!

'Oh, bother!' said Dick. 'Bother and blow and *blast*!'

In the usual way Julian would have told his brother off for using bad language – but Dick's remarks were only too suitable on this occasion!

'Blow and blast it was!' said George, making a brave attempt at a joke. 'You never said a truer word, Dick!'

Julian was sniffing the air around the cistern. 'I don't think it's long since the explosion took place,' he said. 'I can still smell gunpowder. So this theft happened quite recently!'

'Oh, that horrible Justin!' cried Anne, sounding

unusually cross, for her! 'He moved faster than we did.'

'I'm afraid it's my fault,' said Dick. 'I persuaded Peter not to send the police back here. They might have been able to stop Justin in time!'

Timmy seemed to be getting bored with this conversation. He barked, 'Woof! Woof!' Then he ran to the top of the staircase.

'Timmy's right!' said George, following him. 'There's no point in standing about here discussing whose fault it was! What we've got to do now is try to make up for things by telling the police.'

First, of course, they went to see Peter in hospital, because it was only right to let him know what had happened. They were very crestfallen as they told him about the disaster. Peter Darcy wasn't the sort of person to make a big fuss about such things, however. He got the nurse to bring a telephone to his bedside and rang the police station straight away, asking someone to come and take a statement from him.

This time he told the police the full story, and gave them a description of Justin. The police force immediately sprang into action. Road-blocks were set up, and radio messages went out for a watch to be kept on railway stations, seaports and airports.

'My word!' said Anne, rather awed and very much impressed by so much police activity. 'If that doesn't find him, nothing will!'

Unfortunately, she was right. Nothing *did*! Justin seemed to have vanished off the face of the earth, taking the treasure with him!

Several days passed by. Peter's ankle was getting much better. The broken bone was mending nicely, and all would have been well – but for the fact that he had lost the magnificent legacy his grandfather had left him.

'Oh well!' he said philosophically to George and her cousins. 'Money isn't everything, not by a long chalk! I'd much rather have lost that gold than have had anything happen to hurt you kids because of Justin.'

But the children were far from satisfied to let it rest there. They put their heads together and came to a number of conclusions.

'Justin must have guessed that the police would be after him as soon as the theft was discovered,' said Dick. 'So if he hasn't been arrested yet, maybe it means he hasn't tried to make his escape yet either! If you ask me, he's still hiding somewhere quite near here.'

George agreed with her cousin. 'And he probably won't come out of hiding,' she added, 'until all the fuss has died down a bit –'

'And the police aren't being so watchful!' Julian finished her sentence for her.

'Well, if we want to catch him, we'd better act fast!' said Dick, who never gave up easily. 'We must go after him!'

'Hear, hear!' said Anne. 'But *where* must we go after him, Dick?'

'You might as well look for a needle in a haystack!' Peter told them. 'I really don't think there's any point in it, you know, though it's kind of you to worry about my legacy!'

However, George wasn't easily discouraged, any more than her cousin Dick! She was hoping against hope that something would give them a lead.

And she was right to hope, because something *did* give them a lead.

It was market day in Kirrin village, a lovely sunny day, and the children were doing some shopping for Joan again. It wouldn't be long before Aunt Fanny and Uncle Quentin came back home, and Joan wanted to leave them a well-stocked larder! The Five were walking round the market from stall to stall, buying all the things on Joan's long list: fruit, vegetables, butter and eggs. Timmy was enjoying sniffing all the good smells about the place and saying hallo to other dogs he knew.

Anne suddenly stopped dead. 'Look!' she whispered. 'Do you see that man over there, beside the teashop? With a tray of picture postcards slung round his neck?'

'Yes,' said Dick. 'What about him? We often get people walking about selling postcards off a tray in the summer – Kirrin attracts a lot of people who like coming to the seaside for their holidays.'

'That's not what I meant,' said his sister. 'Don't you think he looks like Justin?'

George and the boys looked at the postcard-seller more closely. He was busy giving a woman

her change, and they could see him in profile. He was short, thin and wiry, like Justin, but his hair was cut much shorter, and he had a big handlebar moustache on his upper lip.

'Well, yes, he *is* a bit like Justin – and then again, he isn't!' Julian whispered.

Just then two things happened. First, the man turned in the children's direction. They only just had time to hide behind one of the stalls. And then Timmy, who had been investigating an extremely interesting butcher's stall at the other side of the market-place, came back to find George – and stopped beside the postcard-seller, growling and baring his teeth!

'You see?' said Anne under her breath. 'Timmy recognises him too!'

George whistled quietly. Timmy heard her and came running back to her. Luckily the man didn't seem to have noticed anything. He had just gone up to a group of tourists who had got out of a coach and was offering them his postcards.

Dick was delighted!

'It's him! It's him all right!' he said happily. 'I say, Justin's awfully cunning, isn't he? He camouflaged himself really well! He knew he wouldn't be able to get out of this part of the country very easily – and he can't possibly try selling any of the gold or jewels yet, so he has to make his living somehow! Who would ever suspect an ordinary little postcard-seller in a seaside village?'

84

'Let's go and tell the police,' said Anne.

'Tell the police?' said George. 'Goodness, Anne, we can't do that – he might easily get away while we were at the police station! No, what we've got to do is follow him, and catch him ourselves if possible. After all, there are five of us! The first thing is to follow him and find out where he goes when he leaves the market-place.'

Chapter Eight

SOME NEW DEVELOPMENTS

The 'postcard-seller' had no idea that five pairs of eyes were watching every move he made. He went on offering his wares to passers-by for almost another hour. Then the market people began to take down their stalls, the shoppers were going home, and he covered up his tray of postcards with a sort of lid. It looked as if he was about to leave too.

'We must try to follow him without letting him notice us,' said George under her breath.

She told Timmy that *he* must keep quiet too. The intelligent dog understood, and followed the children in silence, but the bristling hairs on the back of his neck showed how ready he was to attack the man if only she'd give him the word!

Following the postcard-seller was quite easy at first. There were still quite a lot of people out and about, so the children could mingle with them. But then the people thinned out – and Justin left Kirrin village and set out along a little country road. The Five had to be extra careful now if they didn't want him to spot them. They tried to keep under cover of the trees and bushes at the roadside, hurrying from one to another. Once Justin turned round, and they had to jump into the ditch beside the road and lie flat there. Luckily it was summer and the ditch was dry!

At last Justin turned a corner, and they saw that he was making for a tumbledown cottage set a little way back from the road.

The Five saw him open the door. It didn't even seem to be locked.

'If *that's* where he lives, you can bet he's hidden the treasure somewhere else!' whispered Julian. 'Anybody could break into that hovel – easy as pie!'

. 'That just shows how clever Justin's being,' Dick whispered back. 'It looks like an empty place going to ruin, and this is a very lonely spot.'

George didn't say anything. She was concentrating on the really important question. Where *had* Justin hidden Peter Darcy's legacy?

'Well, now we know where his hideout is all we have to do is get him arrested!' she told her cousins. 'You hurry back to the police station! I'll stay here with Timmy and keep watch – we don't want to make the same mistake twice and let Justin slip through our fingers again!'

Julian, Dick and Anne made their way back to

Kirrin, and once they had reached the police station things began to happen very fast! The policemen didn't want to lose any time – they jumped straight into a police car, drove to the deserted cottage and surrounded it. Justin was arrested before he even knew what was happening. How surprised he was!

'Sergeant, you *will* let us know about anything he tells you, won't you?' asked George, a little anxiously.

'I certainly will, Miss Kirrin, and that's a promise!' said the Sergeant, smiling. 'We owe you kids that much!'

And he kept his promise next morning, when George and her cousins called at the police station to see if there was any news.

'Your friend's cousin is remanded in custody in town,' the Sergeant told the children. 'He's being charged with threatening behaviour, illegal possession of a firearm and safe-breaking. Quite a little list! The police officers in town have been questioning him, but I'm afraid they haven't got much out of him. He can't deny breaking into old Mr Darcy's safe, because the fingerprints on its armour-plated door correspond to his. But he refuses to say where he's hidden the gold and jewels he stole.'

'You did search his cottage, didn't you?' said Anne.

'Indeed we did, miss!' said the Sergeant, smiling at the little girl. 'That was the very first step we took! But we didn't find anything, even though we took up the floorboards and dug the soil for quite a large area around the building.'

The children were looking very disappointed.

'Now, don't you worry,' said the kindly Sergeant. 'We're bound to get your friend's property back sooner or later. It's simply a question of time!'

The children hurried off to see Peter. They had been allowed to drop in and see him the night before, just to tell him about Justin's arrest, and he had congratulated them warmly on their success. They only wished they had better news for him now. But he seemed quite cheerful. His ankle was much better, and he could get about on crutches. He was talking of discharging himself from hospital, if the doctor said he could, and moving into his house, Fairfields.

The children could understand his wanting to do that, but obviously he needed someone in the house to look after him while he was still on crutches. When they told dear old Joan about it, she said she thought her cousin Mabel, who lived in Kirrin village, might be able to help. Soon it was all arranged! Mabel said she'd be happy to go and keep house for Peter when he came out of hospital, and that very afternoon the children gave her the keys to Fairfields and she set about giving the place a thorough spring-cleaning – or rather, a thorough summer-cleaning, since it was the middle of August!

'The doctor says I can go home on Monday!' Peter told the children. 'Everyone in the hospital here has been wonderfully kind, but I'll be glad to move into Fairfields all the same. I have such happy memories of visiting my grandfather there when I was a little boy!'

Next day was Sunday, and the Five went back to Justin's cottage to see if they could find any trace of the treasure. They weren't giving up the attempt easily! But hard as they searched the cottage itself and the undergrowth round about, they had no more luck than the police. They found nothing at all!

On Monday they helped Peter Darcy move into Fairfields. Mabel had the house all bright and welcoming for him, and while she was putting his things away he and the Five discussed the question of the missing treasure yet again.

'It *must* be somewhere!' said George. 'And I'm determined to track it down!'

Her cousins felt just the same. So that afternoon they went off to Justin's cottage once more. They felt that if only they went on searching, they just *might* find something – although Peter himself was not very hopeful, and suspected he would never get his property back.

'If *I* were a burglar,' said George, thoughtfully, 'I'm sure I'd want to keep my loot somewhere close – somewhere I could keep an eye on it to make sure it was safe, and where I could gloat over it.'

'What we need is a bulldozer!' sighed Dick, gloomily. 'Then we could dig up the ground really thoroughly for *miles* round the cottage!'

'A bulldozer?' said Julian, laughing. 'Why not an army of woodcutters while you're about it, Dick? Then we could cut down every tree in the little wood! For all we know the treasure's hidden at the top of one of them!'

'I should think it would be quicker to find where it's hidden by sticking a pin in a map!' said Anne.

'Well, go ahead, *stick* pins in a map if you think it'll get you anywhere!' said Dick, laughing at his sister.

'Oh, do stop being so silly, you lot!' said George. 'Here we are, and the best thing –'

Suddenly she stopped dead. The children had indeed reached the deserted spot where Justin's cottage stood – but much to their surprise, they heard voices inside the rickety building. Timmy began to growl, and George made him keep quiet again. Followed by the others, she crept up to one of the cottage windows. Several of its panes were broken.

There were two men inside the cottage, busy searching it!

They were obviously quite sure they were alone, so they didn't take the precaution of keeping their voices down. 'This is maddening!' one of them was saying angrily. 'There's nothing to be found! The police must have been here before us, worse luck!'

'That's right,' agreed the other man. 'Just our

luck that we only heard of Justin's arrest this morning, too! Ozzie, would *you* ever have thought he'd bring off a haul like that?'

The man addressed as Ozzie shook his head, and grunted. 'He's a sly one!' he added. 'Supposed to be mates, aren't we, the three of us? But did he ever breathe a word about this plan of his to us? Not him! Double-crossing us, that was his little game! Wanted to keep it all to himself!'

'Too right he did!' agreed the other man. 'Making off like that – not a word of warning!'

'He did have the police after him, Fred,' said Ozzie.

The man called Fred, who was a hulking, hairy fellow, rather like a gorilla to look at, had been down on all fours searching the floor. He straightened up.

'Ouch! Hard on the back, this crawling about searching! We're just wasting our time, Ozzie. Justin hid the loot somewhere else!'

'Our luck's certainly out! Would've suited us nicely to lay our hands on that little lot just now!'

Julian signed to the others, and the Five silently made their way to the woodland beyond the cottage, following his lead. They hid among the trees.

'We wouldn't have learnt any more, even if we'd stayed there listening,' Julian explained. 'And the longer we stayed, the more risk we ran of them finding us. Look – there they are coming out of the cottage now!'

Sure enough, Ozzie and Fred were setting off down the road towards Kirrin, just as Julian said.

'Oh dear!' sighed Anne. 'I don't like this at *all*! Peter's treasure has disappeared, and even though Justin's been arrested those two men are after it as well as us!'

Anne was right – things had taken a turn for the worse! It wasn't just a matter of looking for the treasure any more. From now on, the Five would have to watch out for those two unsavoury characters who had obviously been Justin's accomplices in other shady dealings!

When they told Peter what they had seen and heard, he did his best to persuade them to stop looking for the treasure, but he got nowhere!

'Give up?' said George, quite shocked. 'The Five *never* give up! Come what may, we're jolly well going to get that treasure back for you!'

'George, that's very nice of you, but I really don't think you'll do it, and I don't want you to try!' said the young man firmly. 'You'd just be running unnecessary risks. As soon as I'm able to get about again properly, I'll be setting off in search of my property myself!'

'But you're still on crutches, so you *can't* get about properly yet,' Dick pointed out. 'And we *can* look for the treasure! I mean, you can't actually stop us, can you?'

Peter had to admit that Dick was right!

'But you will be careful, won't you?' he said anxiously.

'Of course we will!' George promised. Peter looked at her a little suspiciously, and she added innocently, 'We're *always* careful! Particularly me! And I get good intuitions too. I think I've got one now!'

Chapter Nine

TREASURE-HUNTING AGAIN

The others were not so sure about George's intuition. It told her – or so she said – that the treasure really was somewhere near Justin's cottage, and she insisted on dragging the Five back there three days running.

'It simply has to be somewhere here,' she said.

They did try to keep their promise to Peter and be careful. They felt it was very likely that Ozzie and Fred might turn up again, so they left Timmy on guard while they searched. His job was to warn them if any stranger came near.

And Timmy, who was an excellent watchdog, did his job well. The children were busy searching inside the trunks of some hollow trees when he gave them the alarm signal. They just had time to hide in the undergrowth before Ozzie and Fred came in sight. The men had pickaxes with them, and were hacking the ground about here and there, although they didn't seem to be working very methodically. They kept growling angry remarks about 'that double-crossing Justin'.

'There's nothing systematic at all about the way they're searching!' whispered Dick scornfully. 'It'll be a sheer miracle if they find the treasure!'

'Yes — it wouldn't be fair at all, but then life isn't always fair!' Julian pointed out.

But George and Anne had been quick to realise that there was a perfectly simple reason for the foolish way the two men were behaving — they had had rather too much to drink, perhaps so as to encourage themselves to go on with the hard work of searching, and that had made them act in such a stupid, bad-tempered manner!

In spite of all the children's precautions, however, they *did* come face to face with Fred and Ozzie on the morning of the fourth day. It wasn't Timmy's fault. The good dog had spotted someone going along the road, and he galloped off, barking. In fact, the man he had seen was a perfectly innocent passer-by. But while he was giving chase, Fred and Ozzie, who had taken a short cut through the wood, found the children busy searching the surroundings of the cottage yet again. The two men immediately felt very suspicious.

'Hey, what do you kids think you're up to here?' asked Ozzie, in a thick voice which told the children that the men had been drinking again.

'Spying on us, eh?' added Fred.

George's quick wits were hard at work! She looked surprised, and then gave the men a big smile.

'Oh, I see!' she said, laughing. 'You're competing with us, are you? You must be taking part in the treasure hunt too!'

Julian, Dick and Anne looked at their cousin in astonishment. Had George gone right off her head?

The man called Ozzie was looking rather dangerous. He took a step forward.

'Treasure, did you say, my lad?' he inquired, shaking George by the shoulder. 'So you know where it is, do you?'

George looked as innocent as possible.

'Of course not!' she said. 'If we did we wouldn't be looking for it, would we? Oh, sir – the organiser of the treasure hunt said there'd be confetti scattered along the trail – *have* you by any chance seen any confetti lying about? If you have, it would be awfully kind of you to tell us! It wouldn't do you any harm, because the treasure hunt isn't really for grown-ups – and it would help us a lot!'

Fred frowned, and grunted, 'What's the boy talking about?'

By now Dick had realised that George was putting on a clever act! Entering into the spirit of the thing, *he* spoke up.

'Why, the Kirrin Youth Club treasure hunt, of course! And the treasure is a brand new bicycle. So you can see why we're keen to find it if we can!'

Ozzie suddenly looked very relieved and burst out laughing. But he soon sobered down again.

'Right, you kids just get out!' he said, with a dismissive wave of his hand. 'We've had about enough of you! A treasure hunt – ha, ha!' He began laughing again. 'That's a good one!'

The children and Timmy hurried away. But they weren't going to be chased off so easily! They went back to the cottage later that day, in the afternoon.

'It's no good looking where those idiots were fooling about with their pickaxes,' Julian decided. 'Let's try farther away from the cottage. We haven't really explored that bit of the wood over there yet.'

And this time luck was on the children's side! It was George who made the all-important discovery. She suddenly spotted a place at the foot of a big oak tree where the moss was drying up in a rather peculiar way. The area of yellow moss covered a large and distinctly outlined square!

'I say! Come and look at this, everyone!' she called.

Julian, Dick, Anne and Timmy came running up.

'My word, yes! Someone certainly buried something here,' said Julian. 'And then they put the moss back in place – but the weather's been very dry over the last few days, and we've hardly had a drop of rain for ages, so the moss is beginning to die.'

'Oh – could the treasure be down there?' breathed Anne.

'We won't know till we've tried digging!' said the practical Dick. 'I think we'd better come back this evening, when we're least likely to be disturbed. Won't Peter be pleased if we *have* found the treasure!'

'Don't count your chickens before they're hatched,' Julian warned his brother. Feeling in the mood for proverbs, he added, 'There's many a slip 'twixt the cup and the lip' – and ducked to avoid the mock blow Dick aimed at him!

So the Five went back to the wood that evening, armed with spades and pickaxes. They set to work at once, and it wasn't long before Dick's pickaxe struck some metallic object underground.

'Quick!' cried the others. 'Let's see what it is.'

'It' turned out to be a heavy iron chest. The children managed to force open the padlock closing it with the tools they had brought – and once they had lifted the lid they all shouted for joy!

'The gold ingots!' cried Anne happily. 'They *are* here!'

'*And* the precious stones,' said Dick, opening one of the six little boxes that were wedged in between the gold bricks. 'Look, this box is full of diamonds!'

'And this one's full of emeralds,' said George, opening another of the boxes. 'They're all carefully wrapped in cotton wool – well, that's *one* good thing in Justin's favour!'

Julian was the first to stop and think of the practical difficulties that confronted them now. 'Listen, we can't just take the ingots away,' he said. 'They're too heavy. We'll have to leave them where they are for the moment – and Peter can ask the police to come and pick them up in a van, or something. But we _can_ take the precious stones. They're easy enough to carry!'

So the children put the little boxes in their pockets, and then covered up the iron chest with soil again. They were just finishing the job when they heard Timmy barking frantically.

'Quick!' said Julian. 'There's somebody coming!'

But although their spades fairly flew, the children weren't quite quick enough! They were still shovelling earth back when Ozzie and Fred loomed up before them, looking very threatening!

'Oho!' said Ozzie. 'Digging for that bicycle, are you? You won't get us to swallow _that_ story again in a hurry!'

George was thinking fast – and she suddenly saw how she could still lead Ozzie and Fred astray. Whatever happened, the two men mustn't know that the children had been burying the iron chest again _after_ opening it! She must get them to believe that she and her cousins had only just begun to dig. And to make the story she was going to tell seem more likely, she decided to stick to the treasure-hunt tale she had told the men before.

'Well, we _are_ digging for the bicycle in a way!' she said with a friendly smile. 'You see, we're hoping to dig up a tin box containing a note which says whoever takes it back to the Youth Club will get the new bicycle – it's first prize in the big annual treasure hunt, you see!'

Dick backed her up. 'You wouldn't want to keep us from winning it, would you, sir?' he said,

sounding very anxious. 'I mean, what could *you* do with a child's bike?'

But Ozzie was still suspicious. 'You kids just stay right where you are!' he said. 'Fred, keep an eye on them. I'm going to do a bit of digging!'

'You've got no right to steal the note about the bicycle!' said Julian indignantly, entering into the spirit of the thing. 'It's for my little sister here – at least, we want to win it for her, you see! She really *does* need a new bike so much! Don't you, Anne?'

'Oh yes!' said Anne, in a very pathetic voice.

Timmy was longing to leap on the men, but George knew that they were not really in a very strong position, and she whispered an order to her dog to make him keep still.

It wasn't long before Ozzie had dug up the iron chest again. Luckily he was so pleased that he didn't notice the padlock had been forced! He and Fred shouted for joy when they opened it and saw all the gold. Anne thought this was a good moment for her to make a contribution to the game the Five were playing.

'Oh dear!' she said, sounding disappointed. 'It isn't the box with the treasure in it after all!'

That made the two men roar with laughter. But then they suddenly stopped laughing, and looked at the children in a way that gave them shivers down the back.

'Hm – if we're going to take this gold away with us, I reckon we ought to get rid of these nosey kids!' muttered Fred.

Chapter Ten

LASSOES TO THE RESCUE

'Well, it won't be difficult to keep *them* out of the way!' said Ozzie. 'All we have to do is truss them up like chickens – and they're going to provide us with the rope to do it themselves!'

He pointed to the lassoes Dick and George were carrying coiled up and attached to their belts. Then he and Fred made the children stand in pairs, back to back, and tied each pair together with one of the lassoes.

As for Timmy, Fred attached his collar to the rope tying Julian and Anne up, and when the dog barked, he said threatingly, 'Any more of that and I silence him for good with this pickaxe!'

George could have murdered *him* for saying that, but she told Timmy to keep quiet. There was nothing the Five could do! They had to stand by and watch while the two men finished digging up the iron chest.

'The gold's here all right – but didn't the news-papers say there were precious stones too?' asked Ozzie suddenly.

'That's right,' Fred told him. 'But they're not here, so I suppose that so-and-so Justin has gone and hidden them somewhere else, to be on the safe side.

'Just our luck!' said Ozzie gloomily.

'Cheer up, mate!' said Fred. 'There's plenty here to keep us in luxury for the rest of our days!'

'Yeah . . . but we still have to get the gold away, and it's heavy. You go and get the van from the lane where we left it, while I deal with these kids!'

George and her cousins shivered yet again. They had thought they were simply going to be tied up – the idea of being 'dealt with' didn't sound nice at all. They were certainly witnesses who could do the two men a good deal of harm – could Fred and Ozzie actually be planning to kill them?

It wasn't quite as bad as that. While Fred went to fetch their van, Ozzie made the children walk to the cottage. They could only take small, shuffling steps, because their ankles were tied together. Once they were inside, Ozzie told them to lie down on the floor, and he tied the ropes more tightly.

'You're going to stay here like good, quiet children until someone turns up to free you. And you can think yourselves lucky if *that* happens before you die of starvation!'

The children did not enjoy the next few minutes at all. Ozzie went out, closing the door behind him.

105

Then they heard Fred drive up in a noisy van, and they realised that he and Ozzie must be loading the chest of gold ingots into it.

But the worst was yet to come! Instead of driving straight off with their loot, the men came back into the cottage, picked up some old planks which were lying about in a corner, and went out of doors again.

'Fetch a hammer and some nails – you'll find them in the toolbox in the van,' Ozzie told his companion. Then he raised his voice for the children's benefit, and told them, 'We're going to board up the door and the window! Can't be too careful, can we? I don't want you escaping too soon!'

The blows of the hammer were a loud and dismal sound to the children's ears. They were all thinking that old Joan probably wouldn't realise they were not at Kirrin Cottage until next morning. When she did, she would get in touch with Peter Darcy, and no doubt the two of them would go to the police and tell them about the cottage – but by that time Ozzie, Fred and the gold would be far away. There was no police watch out for Justin's two former accomplices! Would anything ever be seen of them and their loot again? The Five felt they had failed just when it looked as if they were going to recover Peter's property for him! The one thing that cheered them up a little was the thought of the boxes of jewels in their pockets.

Outside the cottage, the van started up. The children could hear the sound of its engine dying away in the distance. Silence fell. Night had fallen too, and it was pitch dark inside the cottage.

Poor little Anne was sniffling. Timmy was half choking himself in his efforts to get free. 'Well, *now* we're in a nice mess!' muttered George angrily.

'There's one good thing – our friends Fred and Ozzie didn't think of searching us!' Dick pointed out.

'That's true,' Julian agreed. 'We can at least give Peter the diamonds and emeralds back. You could say we've only half failed!'

'Yes,' said Anne, miserably. 'But we're still prisoners here!'

Suddenly they heard a sharp snapping noise, followed by a yelp from Timmy. The poor dog had been struggling so hard that he had broken his collar. Caught off balance, he went sprawling on the ground.

'Oh, well *done*, Timmy!' cried George. She was delighted when her faithful friend picked himself up and came over to lick her cheek. 'Listen, everyone – Timmy's got free. Timmy, now you must help us free ourselves too!'

She and Dick were tied together so tightly that they could hardly breathe – it was high time for Timmy to come to the rescue. Luckily he had very good, strong teeth, and he didn't take long to understand what his little mistress wanted him to do. She only had to tell him, 'Bite, Timmy! Good dog! Bite!' and he set to work on the rope she was holding out as close to his mouth as she could. This was a trick she had trained Timmy to do, and he put up a very good performance now, when it mattered most!

Gradually, he chewed his way through the rope, and at last it fell apart. After that it didn't take George and Dick long to untie the rest of their bonds. George gave Timmy a great big thank-you kiss on his nose, and then made haste to help Dick untie Julian and Anne too.

Soon the children were standing side by side in the cottage. 'If only it wasn't so dark we could probably find some way to get out of here,' said Julian.

And suddenly, as if in answer to his wish, the cottage was flooded with silvery light! For a moment the children were staggered – then George began to laugh, and pointed to the roof. There was a big hole in it, and the moon, which had just come out from behind a cloud, was shining through this hole, as if it wanted a closer look at the young prisoners.

'Well, you wanted light and you've got it, Ju!' said George. 'What's more, the moon is showing us our way of escape too! Isn't that kind of it!'

'You're right,' said Julian. 'We can get out through the roof!'

'But how?' said Anne doubtfully. 'It looks an awfully long way up!'

'We'll use our lassoes, of course!' cried Dick.

He picked up the two ropes and tied them together. Then he deftly threw one end of the double-length rope he had made over one of the beams sticking out by the hole in the roof.

George couldn't help laughing. 'I say – Fred and Ozzie weren't as clever as they thought!' she said. 'They dealt with the door and the window, but they forgot the ceiling! Come on, then, let's climb up! This is rather like the way we got out of our compartment when the train was derailed – so we've had practice!'

She was the first to climb the rope. Once she was on the roof, she hauled Timmy up to join her. Dick climbed the rope next, and then Anne. Anne was a little scared, but Julian stood down below and promised to catch her if she fell, so of course she didn't. Julian himself went up the rope last.

The lasso was equally useful for getting them down off the roof, too. They tied it to a beam on the edge of the roof, and they all climbed down it. Finally, Dick managed to wriggle it off the end of the beam, get it down to the ground and coil it up again – he and George didn't want to lose their good lassoes.

The whole escape had been quite quick. The Five wasted no time, but set off for Fairfields as fast as they could go. When they reached the house, they *fell* rather than *got* off their bicycles and rang the front door-bell, loud and long.

Mabel, who had just dropped off to sleep, finally came to open the door. 'What can Joan be thinking

of?' she grumbled. 'Fancy letting you children roam round the village at this hour of the night!'

Peter Darcy came out of his bedroom, wearing pyjamas, leaning on his crutches, and looking very worried. His face cleared when he saw the children safe and sound.

'My word, you gave me a shock!' he said. 'When I didn't see or hear anything of you all evening, I was afraid something disastrous must have happened!'

'Well – I'm afraid something disastrous *has* happened,' Julian confessed. 'Or *half* of something disastrous, anyway! But here's the good half of our news first. Look – your precious stones!'

And before Peter's surprised and delighted eyes, the children brought out the little boxes full of diamonds and emeralds. Then they told him the whole story of their adventure. Peter began thanking them for all they had done, but George wouldn't let him.

'Peter, my father will be home tomorrow,' she said, interrupting him. 'I'll ask him to come to Fairfields and see you, and I'm sure he'll drive you to the bank in his car. Then all you have to do is hire a bank vault, and your precious stones will be perfectly safe. As for the ingots –'

It was Peter's turn to interrupt. 'As for the ingots, it's up to the police to find them!' he said firmly. 'You four have done quite enough – you five, I mean, counting Timmy. I don't like the thought of this last adventure of yours one bit.

Those two men could easily have treated you even worse. I absolutely forbid you to go exposing yourselves to any more danger!'

The young Canadian was quite pale. He was obviously upset and horrified at the thought of the risks the children had been running for him. Anne gave him one of her sweetest smiles.

'Please don't worry about us, Peter!' she told him. 'As you said –'

'– it's really the business of the police to find the men and make them cough up your gold!' Dick finished for her.

'Yes, exactly!'

A little later, on their way back to Kirrin Cottage, George said crossly to her cousins Dick and Anne, 'Whatever made you tell Peter we were giving up? Personally, I've got no intention of doing any such thing! *I'm* carrying on to the bitter end – and I already have the glimmerings of an idea!'

George usually did have the glimmerings of an idea in her head – or even more than one! But before she could tell her cousins what this one was, Dick protested, 'I never said we were giving up!' And he laughed. 'I just let Peter *think* so – sort of to calm him down! Otherwise he'd have thrown a fit, and I expect he'd have got Uncle Quentin to forbid us to make any more inquiries into the disappearance of the ingots – and you know what Uncle Quentin's like when anybody disobeys him!'

'Oh, *that's* all right, then!' said George, smiling at him. 'Yes, now I come to think of it, you didn't really promise anything! Well done!'

Julian was looking a little worried. 'George, about this idea of yours,' he began. 'What is it, exactly? Sometimes your ideas are a bit – well, wild!'

The children had reached Kirrin Cottage and were dismounting from their cycles. 'You'll find out, all in good time!' said George, opening the garden gate very quietly. 'I'll tell you in the morning. Just at the moment the important thing is to get indoors without letting Joan know we've been out all evening! It *is* late, too. I'm asleep on my feet! How about you, Timmy?'

The good dog gave a very quiet bark. He seemed to understand that he mustn't wake Joan.

The Five slept soundly until morning, and they had a ravenous appetite at breakfast time. Joan was quite surprised when they came to ask for second helpings of sausages, mushrooms and tomatoes, and they polished off a whole loaf of bread too, with butter and honey. Feeling pleasantly full, they went out into the garden.

'Now, let's hear your idea, George!' Julian, Dick and Anne asked.

George was perfectly ready to tell them now. All right, here goes!' she said. 'I think we ought to try to put ourselves in the thieves' place. After they took the ingots yesterday, I should think they'd have just one thing on their minds: getting their loot to a safe place, and lying low somewhere themselves to wait for the hue and cry to die down.'

'Well, that's obvious!' said Julian.

'Right. Well, if Ozzie and Fred had any sense, that's what they'd do, and they'd leave it at that. But as we know, they *haven't* got much sense! Remember the stupid way they behaved? And people who are greedy as well as stupid are very likely to do something rash!'

'What are you getting at?' asked Dick.

'Just this – I guess those two idiots will stop to think it over, and what they'll tell themselves is that since they found Justin's gold ingots they might easily find the precious stones too. So they'll come back and start searching round that cottage again – taking precautions, of course – and then –' Here George stopped for a moment, looking at her cousins with a gleam in her eye. 'And then I'll be there, waiting for them! We'll keep watch on the cottage, and when our friends turn up again, we'll tell the police and get them arrested. All right?'

'All *right*!' agreed Julian, Dick and Anne fervently, and in chorus.

'Woof!' said Timmy, in such a loud voice that it shook Joan's saucepans in the kitchen!

The Five started keeping watch on the cottage and its immediate surroundings that very day. It was likely to be a long and tedious job, but they were determined not to miss anything – they were even willing to give up some of the bathing and games on the beach they enjoyed so much.

Aunt Fanny and Uncle Quentin, back from London, were slightly surprised to find that the Five had a new craze – a craze for picnics! They went out all day, every day, taking a picnic with them. Peter Darcy had his suspicions, but the children were careful not to let him know what they were really up to.

Every evening, after supper, they managed to slip out of the house and go back to the cottage, and they stayed there as long as they could. When they came home at last, late at night, they felt disappointed, because for four whole days nothing happened. They were having a very boring time, and their tempers were wearing thin. George's cousins began to think that just for once her idea hadn't been particularly bright.

But at last, late in the afternoon of the fourth day, the children heard Timmy give a low growl of warning. They quickly hid on the outskirts of the little wood – and saw two men approaching. Two men who, at first sight, seemed to be ragged, disreputable-looking tramps.

When they looked more closely, however, there was no doubt about it. The two tramps were Ozzie and Fred in disguise!

Chapter Eleven

OUTWITTING FRED AND OZZIE

'It's them!' whispered George, triumphantly. 'I was right!'

'Ssh!' Julian told her. 'They're looking round very suspiciously – this is no moment to give ourselves away! Oh, good, they're going into the cottage. I'm sure they'll stay to search it, so now's our time to go to the police station!'

That was certainly the most sensible thing to do, and the Five were just about to turn and set off for Kirrin village and the police when Ozzie came out of the cottage and walked into the wood. He passed within a few feet of the children as they hid among the undergrowth, and disappeared into the trees.

'Oh, blow!' exclaimed Dick. 'They've separated! We didn't expect them to do that – and now if we go and tell the police, they may only catch one of them!'

'Yes,' said Anne sadly. 'That's torn it!'

'Oh no, it hasn't!' said George firmly. 'We just have to think up a new plan of campaign, that's all – and fast! Meanwhile, we mustn't lose track of Ozzie. Timmy, that's your job! Follow that man, and don't let him see you! Follow him – follow and hide!'

Timmy really was a most intelligent dog. His mistress had trained him to understand certain commands and obey them at once. Wagging his tail, he set off straight away after Ozzie.

'Actually, it may be quite useful if they've separated,' George whispered to her cousins. 'As luck will have it, we're going to be four against one so far as poor old Fred's concerned! He doesn't suspect a thing!'

'You mean we're going to attack him all together?' said Dick. 'And overpower him?'

'I don't see why not,' said Julian thoughtfully. He was a cautious boy – but he was also big and strong for his age, and George's plan seemed quite feasible.

The children came out of the wood and crept stealthily towards the cottage. They could hear the sound of a pickaxe coming from inside it.

'That's a good thing,' whispered Anne. 'The noise will cover the sound of our footsteps.'

But there was an unwelcome surprise awaiting the children. When they looked through the window of the cottage, they could see Fred had taken a pickaxe out of his tramp's bundle and was working away with it – but facing the door the whole time. If they attacked him he'd be bound to see them coming, and that pickaxe looked as if it could be quite a dangerous weapon.

This time it was Julian who had an idea. 'The roof!' he whispered. 'The hole in the roof! We could get in that way!'

Dick was already giving George a leg up. Once she was on the roof she tied her lasso to the beam they had used before, and her cousins climbed up after her one by one. Down below, Fred was still hacking away with his pickaxe, whistling while he worked. He hadn't heard anything at all.

'Now what?' asked Anne softly.

Julian was peering down through the hole in the roof. 'It's not really much of a drop,' he whispered. 'I suggest we all let ourselves down at the same time, on top of Fred – he'll break our fall. And let's hope Ozzie's too far off to hear him when he shouts!'

'No – I've got a better idea!' said George. 'Let's *lasso* Fred! I'm pretty sure I can get him – and if the rest of you help me, we can pull him up! Like pulling a fish out of the water!'

'Good idea!' said Dick. 'And if you do happen to miss then we can still drop down on him, if we move fast.'

Fred suddenly stopped swinging his pickaxe. He was standing directly below the children. He put the pickaxe down, and took a large checked handkerchief out of his pocket to mop the sweat from his face.

'Now's our moment!' breathed Julian. 'Go on, George! Good luck!'

George's lasso whistled down through the hole in the roof. Fred looked up – and the children could see the astonishment on his face when he spotted them perched there above him. At that very moment the running noose of the lasso caught him and tightened round his chest under his armpits. He tried to struggle free, but it was no use! The rope was pulling at him, and there was nothing he could do about it. Up above, clinging on to the end of it like grim death, the four cousins were hauling away together!

Fred's feet left the ground. The united efforts of the children managed to raise him a little way into the air.

But he was a heavy man – and he was beginning to struggle in earnest now. 'Quick!' said Julian, between his teeth. 'Let's tie the rope to the beam!'

A moment later Fred was dangling from the end of the lasso with his chest caught fast in the rope. The more he struggled, the tighter he pulled the running noose!

Dick burst out laughing. 'I wouldn't do that if I were you, old chap!' he advised Fred. 'This place is rather rickety – if you shake the beam hard enough it *might* give way, but then again, you might well get the whole roof coming down on your head. So I think you'd better keep still until we come back for you. And it's no use shouting, because there's nobody else around!'

The cousins used Dick's lasso to help them get down from the roof again. Once they were on the ground they held a hasty consultation.

'What do we do now?' Anne asked the other three.

'That's obvious!' Dick told her. 'You cycle off and tell the police what's going on, Anne! You can show them the way to the cottage and let them take delivery of one nicely trussed Fred!'

'I think Julian had better stay here to guard our prisoner,' said George. 'We don't want him escaping. Meanwhile you and I will go after Timmy and try to capture Ozzie, Dick.'

'Oh no, you don't!' said Julian firmly. 'For one thing, the pair of you could never overpower Ozzie, even with Timmy to help you. For another, we've got Fred perfectly helpless in there. He won't get away! And we could even do with Anne's help, too, if we're going to take Ozzie prisoner.'

George thought fast. 'I suppose you're right,' she said. 'And Ozzie just might slip through our fingers between the time Anne had reached the police station and the time the police arrived – in which case he might get back to the cottage and set his accomplice free.'

'Good thinking,' said Dick. 'So we'll all stay together – but let's hurry up! Ozzie, here we come!'

And the children set off the same way as Ozzie had gone.

After they had gone a hundred metres or so through the wood, George stopped and began whistling like a blackbird. Her cousins stood perfectly still beside her, waiting, but nothing happened.

'I hope we're on the right track!' George muttered. 'Right – let's go on!'

After another fifty metres, George stopped to whistle again, but still there was no response.

'Oh, bother!' she said. 'Ozzie can't have gone to dig *very* far off! Let's try over to the right a bit.'

The four cousins changed direction and turned right. In a few moments, George whistled for the third time. And a second or so later there was a slight noise in the undergrowth, and Timmy's hairy head came into view. The good dog jumped up at his mistress, licking her lovingly all over her face, but he didn't bark – because when he was on 'active service' he knew he must keep quiet. George patted him, smiling.

'So there you are, Timmy! Good boy!' she told him. 'I can tell you've done what I wanted. Good dog! Right – show us the way! Lead, Timmy! Lead!'

Timmy immediately turned round and plunged into the trees, with Julian, George, Dick and Anne following him in silence.

The dog had come running to meet them, but he slackened his pace as he led them back the way he had come, turning round now and then to make sure they were still behind him.

It wasn't long before he stopped, with one paw raised in the air. His ears were pricked. At that very moment the children heard the sound of a tool hacking away at the ground.

Craning their necks, they saw their quarry! There was Ozzie, bare to the waist, his muscular arms wielding a large pickaxe. Chunks of earth were flying up from it as it hit the ground.

He was digging in the shade of a big oak tree, not very far from the one where the Five had discovered the iron chest containing the gold and jewels.

'I wonder why he's digging under that *particular* tree,' whispered Anne.

'It's just chance, I expect,' Dick told her. 'He's got to look somewhere, hasn't he?'

'Ssh!' said Julian. 'Don't talk so much.'

George moved a few yards farther off, signing to the others and Timmy to follow her. 'But we do have to talk, all the same,' she said. 'We've got to decide on a plan of action – go ahead, but keep your voices down. I don't think Ozzie can hear us from where he's digging.'

'All right,' said Julian. 'Plan of action! Well, what do *you* suggest, George? I can't think of anything except all of us rushing him at once!'

'That's what we thought of doing with Fred,' Dick reminded his brother. 'But Ozzie's rather heftier than Fred. Did you see his muscles? I wouldn't have thought he was so strong.'

'Listen,' said George. 'Why don't we lasso him, just as we lassoed Fred?'

Julian looked at his cousin a little ironically. 'For

the very good reason that we haven't got a roof or a beam with us!' he pointed out.

'You're right there,' said George, not at all disconcerted. 'We haven't got a beam, but we've got something even better!' And she pointed at the tree where Ozzie was hard at work. 'A branch of that oak would do the trick, wouldn't it?'

'George, don't be silly!' Julian begged her. 'We'd have to pass Ozzie at close quarters to get up there.'

'Not necessarily. First we climb that tree – just nearby – and then we go on to the next tree, and then the one after that, and so on till we get to the big oak and Ozzie!'

'Thinking of joining a circus as a trapeze artiste, are you? Come off it, George!' said Julian.

'No, honestly, Ju, it *would* work!' his cousin assured him. 'All these trees are oaks – they've got good strong branches, and they won't break under our weight. What's more, they're growing so close that their branches are all tangled up with each other. We've all got a good head for heights, and this is as safe a way to get where we want as any other.'

'But how do we get up in the first place?' asked Julian. He still sounded doubtful. 'The lowest branch of this oak is much too high for us to jump up!'

'You're forgetting Dick's lasso,' said George.

Dick liked his cousin's idea. He uncoiled his lasso and threw it – and in a moment he and

George were climbing up to the tree. Julian, Anne and Timmy didn't follow them – they stayed on the ground, ready to rush in once Ozzie had been lassoed.

And now Dick and George began their circus act on the high wire! It really *was* a bit risky. But they were both nimble and athletic, and they managed to leap from branch to branch and then from tree to tree without too much difficulty.

Anne was holding her breath. George and Dick soon disappeared from sight, hidden by the oak leaves.

'Let's get a bit closer,' Julian whispered. 'The nearer we can get to Ozzie the faster we'll be able to act when the time comes.'

Followed by Timmy, they were only a few metres from Ozzie when things started to happen with a vengeance!

Dick had reached the branches of the oak tree just above Ozzie, and he was about to throw his lasso when his foot suddenly slipped on the branch where he was standing.

He let out a squeal, and fell out of the tree head first!

Other voices cried out too – the voices of George, who was still up in the tree, of Julian and Anne, who were hiding behind a bush and watching in alarm – and the voice of Ozzie himself as Dick landed right on his back! Both of them rolled over on the ground.

So much for George's plan of action! It looked as

if all was lost – but it wasn't, not quite yet.

George realised that they must take advantage of the fact that Ozzie had been taken by surprise. She let herself drop out of the oak tree too, and landed on Ozzie's shoulders just as he was getting up again. Julian and Anne were already running to help the others. As for Timmy, he was barking as if he were giving a war-cry! He had his teeth firmly planted in Ozzie's leg. Dick had been stunned by his fall, but only for a moment, and he too jumped at Ozzie.

But Ozzie was a big, strong man. He shook the children off, dealing them several heavy blows, and bent to retrieve his pickaxe. It would be a terrible weapon in his huge hands!

However, Timmy wasn't going to give him time to use it! Just as Ozzie bent over to pick it up, turning his back to the dog, Timmy jumped! He got the waistband of the man's trousers between his teeth and pulled for all he was worth. Ozzie wasn't wearing a belt, and Timmy was pulling so hard that the buttons of his waistband popped off. His trousers began to fall revealing a pair of pink underpants.

It was so comical that Anne couldn't help laughing. As for Ozzie, he automatically reached for his trousers to stop them slipping further, forgetting all about the pickaxe. He glanced at the children in dismay. They thought they'd never seen anything so funny in their lives – such a big man looking so embarrassed!

But George was quick to take advantage of his momentary embarrassment. She grabbed the pickaxe. And Timmy returned to the attack, feeling very proud of himself. Poor Ozzie! He didn't know what to do next. He was holding up his trousers with one hand and trying to fend Timmy off with the other. George was threatening him with the pickaxe. Julian, Dick and Anne had armed themselves with stout branches, and they were looking very menacing too.

'I think you'd better come quietly, you know!' George told the thief. 'Stand still and let us tie you up – or I'll tell my dog here to make mincemeat of you, and you know what *he* can do!'

She was waving the pickaxe in the air and looking very fierce – so one way and another, Ozzie thought he had better do as she said! He surrendered, and the boys had him tied up with Dick's lasso before you could say Jack Robinson!

The policemen at Kirrin police station could hardly believe their eyes when the Five turned up that evening, escorting two bound prisoners! They solemnly handed Ozzie and Fred over. And it wasn't long before Ozzie and Fred told the police where they had hidden the gold ingots – in a disused barn which stood in an isolated country spot.

Night was falling when Julian, Dick, George and Anne rang the doorbell at Fairfields.

'You again?' said Mabel.

'Yes – but we've got *good* news this time!' said

Dick. 'Peter!' he shouted. 'Peter! Where are you?'

Peter came downstairs as fast as he could – leaning on a stick and not crutches now. George told him all about their latest adventure and its happy ending, and the young Canadian's eyes filled with tears.

'I *knew* you were good kids!' was all he could say.

The four cousins felt they had to protest modestly – but Timmy said, 'Woof!' very firmly, and obviously that meant, 'Yes!'